"Perhaps we should be drinking to the end of Marquis." Madeline put down her glass and stepped forward to lean against Carol. "I'm frightened." She gave a self-deprecatory laugh. "Terrified, actually."

Carol put down her glass so she could hold her. "You'll be safe as long as you're careful. It'll just be for a while. He'll make a mistake and we'll catch him."

"Promise?"

"I promise I'll do everything I can."

Madeline tilted her head to look up at Carol's face. Her gray eyes were wide, her mouth inviting. "Did you know fear is the ultimate aphrodisiac, Carol? It's well-documented that in life-threatening situations perfect strangers will fall upon each other and make love."

"We're not perfect strangers."

A long, slow kiss. The trembling began deep within Carol. She wanted to forget all the tensions and failures of her life. To just live for this moment, to accept what Madeline had to offer, even if there were unspoken conditions attached.

DOUBLE BLUFF

THE 7TH DETECTIVE INSPECTOR CAROL ASHTON MYSTERY

Claire McNab

THE NAIAD PRESS, INC.
1995

Printed in the United States of America on acid-free paper
First Edition

Editor: Christine Cassidy
Cover designer: Bonnie Liss (Phoenix Graphics)
Typesetter: Sandi Stancil

Library of Congress Cataloging-in-Publication Data

McNab, Claire.
   Double bluff : a Carol Ashton mystery / by Claire McNab.
     p.   cm.
   ISBN 1-56280-096-5 (pbk.)
   I. Title.
PS3563.C3877D68   1995
813'.54—dc20   95-14534
                                   CIP

To Sheila

About the Author

Claire McNab is the author of seven Detective Inspector Carol Ashton mysteries: *Lessons in Murder, Fatal Reunion, Death Down Under, Cop Out, Dead Certain, Body Guard* and *Double Bluff.* She has also written two romances, *Under the Southern Cross* and *Silent Heart.* While a high school English teacher in Sydney she began her writing career with comedy plays and textbooks. In her native Australia she is known for her self-help and children's books.

For reasons of the heart, Claire is now a permanent resident of the United States, although she tries to visit Australia at least once a year and warmly recommends her country as a breathtaking vacation destination.

Books by Claire McNab

*Lessons in Murder**

*Fatal Reunion**

*Death Down Under**

*Cop Out**

*Dead Certain**

*Body Guard**

*Double Bluff**

Under the Southern Cross

Silent Heart

* Detective Inspector Carol Ashton mysteries

PROLOGUE

My Madeline,
You haven't given me that special, private smile
lately, and you know I've been watching every show.
And when I turned on the set Friday night you
weren't there. I don't want to see that bitch Kimberley
filling in for you again. I want you.
Where were you? You never said you wouldn't be
there. I don't like that. Not telling the truth can hurt
you, hurt you so much.

Pain is so hot, isn't it? Feelings and sounds. From shrieks to a final whimper. Delicious.

Marquis

CHAPTER ONE

"Stalkers fall into three categories," said Carol. "First is the rejected lover — someone you had a personal relationship with, but told to get lost."

Madeline Shipley leaned back in the dressing room chair submitting to the ministrations of a makeup woman. "All my rejected lovers are delighted to be rejected. What's the second sort?"

Carol watched as Madeline's copper hair was brushed into sleek curves to accent the symmetry of her face. "Second is the stranger stalker, who's simply doing it for crime — rape, robbery, that sort of thing."

"Nothing so normal. I'd say this guy's getting a real charge out of it — first flowers with a note, and now he's writing letters to me."

"Therefore, as is entirely appropriate, this one's in the third category, the celebrity stalker."

Madeline grinned at Carol's dry tone. "You're a celebrity in your own right, Carol. You can have a stalker of your own."

Irritated by her levity, Carol said coolly, "It isn't anything to laugh about. Whoever it is has a relationship with you only in his head, but to him it's absolutely real, although he may never have actually met you."

A promo for Madeline's show flashed on the screen of the on-air monitor mounted above the makeup mirrors. Chin high, gray eyes wide, she stared soberly from the screen. The voice-over was muted, but Carol had heard the familiar words often enough: "At seven the award-winning Shipley Report! Madeline Shipley brings you the news behind the news . . . the stories, the information, the insights you *must* have for today's changing world . . ."

"I'll finish. Thanks, June," said Madeline to the makeup woman. When they were alone she leaned forward to check her teeth for lipstick, then smiled provocatively at Carol's reflection in the mirror. "You're looking good, darling. Of course, I've always had a weakness for blondes."

Carol refused to be deflected. "You called me because you said you wanted my advice."

Madeline's smile faded. "I do." She rummaged in

a blue leather briefcase beside the chair. "This one came in the mail today. I saved the envelope too. It was posted locally." As she handed Carol the typed letter enclosed in a plastic sleeve she added, "And aren't I smart to think about fingerprints?"

Carol was frowning over the letter. "You're brilliant," she said absently.

"He's getting a bit tiresome, whoever he is. I've had obsessive fans before, of course. And I suppose it's exaggerating to say he's a stalker — he's only written to me."

"He could be watching you, too."

"You make me feel so secure, Carol."

"And there have only been letters? No phone calls?"

"Everything's been in writing and he always signs himself Marquis. The first ones got thrown out, but once I realized I might have a genuine fruitcake writing to me, I got Jim to start a file."

"Jim?"

Madeline made a face at her. "If you *ever* went to the trouble of coming to the station, you'd know Jim Borlie was my new personal assistant. Would you believe Jim and I went to school together? We'd lost touch, but he contacted me a few weeks ago and I gave him a job. Anyway, he'll be here in a minute to brief me on any last-minute changes, so you can meet him." She passed over a black folder. "Here are the rest of the letters. You will stay, won't you? We can have dinner afterwards."

"I don't know, Madeline, I'm very busy . . ."

Madeline carefully removed the tissues protecting the neckline of her tailored pale green dress from the heavy studio makeup. "You always seem to get the high profile cases. I can't imagine why they don't assign you to some ordinary, grubby little murder for a change."

Carol grimaced. "I wish they would. Tala Orlando's death has the media sharks in a feeding frenzy."

"I can't believe she killed herself." Madeline swung around in her chair, her expression somber. "At the dinner party the night before she died she was in great form. Suicide seems so out of character. I'm sure it was a stupid, pointless accident. Don't you think so?"

"I don't know yet." Carol knew that many people who later committed suicide would exhibit quite cheerful behavior after they had made a firm decision to die because they felt relief that their emotional suffering was going to end.

"Or you're not saying." Madeline was clearly exasperated.

Of course Tala Orlando's death would have been big news at any time, but as it had been a particularly slow news week, the media excitement had been even more frenzied when her body had been found, seated in the front seat of her burgundy Rolls, its engine still purring reliably, in her locked garage. MEDIA MOGUL'S MYSTERY DEATH, the headlines had screamed.

It could have been a standard suicide, but the evidence wasn't conclusive and persistent rumors that there was something sinister about her death had kept interest in the case hot. That afternoon Carol had attended a media briefing where she had made calming "our inquiries are continuing" noises to impatient reporters.

The media interest was understandable. Tala Orlando had been a larger-than-life personality with a rags-to-riches career as an independent television producer. Now, Carol thought soberly, she was chilled flesh in the morgue refrigerator, waiting for Carol to decide whether a crime had been committed and when to release her body to the family.

Madeline put her hand on Carol's arm. "Tala and I were friends, even though professionally we were at war over the time slot for her new quiz show. She was so vital — I have trouble believing I'll never see her again."

"I can't say you'll be the first to know, but I'll tell you when there's something concrete."

"Why do I bother cultivating you, Carol?" Madeline's tone was sardonic. "You never give me an exclusive on *anything*. I mean, one of my best friends dies, and you won't even give me any details, in spite of the fact *I've* answered every question you asked about her."

"Could it be that the *Shipley Report* will be doing a special on Tala Orlando? Is that why you want to pump me?"

Anger flashed across Madeline's face. "Look, Carol, I'm not pumping you for information to put in some program. I was close to Tala and I'm terribly upset that she's gone. I miss her and I don't understand how she could have died. That's why I want to know."

Embarrassed by her own cynicism, Carol said placatingly, "Forgive me, but it seems everybody

7

wants to get the inside word." Wanting to change the subject, she picked up the black folder Madeline had given her. "Who's touched these letters?"

"Just Jim and me." Madeline looked a little smug. "You'll be wanting to fingerprint us both, I know."

"I won't be involved, Madeline. This should go to the locals. I'll call and make sure they take it seriously."

Madeline was obviously taken aback. "But I expected *you* to do something about it . . ."

"I'm sorry. It just isn't possible." Carol flipped over a page in the folder. "It could be someone who has a grudge against you. How about your ex-husband?"

"He's not ex, Carol. We're separated. Permanently. I just haven't got around to divorcing him." She stood to brush any specks of makeup from her dress. "I don't think for a moment it's Paul sending these letters. He's overseas, and besides, it's not his style."

"Have you spoken lately?"

"No, and I don't intend to. We've got nothing to say to each other and —"

She broke off as there was a soft knock at the door. The soft-bodied man with rounded shoulders came into the dressing room. He smiled broadly when he saw Carol. "Inspector Ashton! I'm Jim Borlie." He shook her hand warmly. "It's great to meet you. Frankly, I've admired you from afar for years." He looked at the folder in her hands. "Madeline's told you about our little problem with the letters."

"I'll taking them for analysis."

She regarded him with interest. Jim Borlie was new at the station, and Carol automatically considered him as a possible source of the letters.

Even if Madeline had gone to school with him, she couldn't know what he was like now. Neatly dressed in tan slacks and a blue pullover, he was about Carol's height but with disproportionately small hands and feet for a man. He had wide-set brown eyes and very even white teeth that made his smile particularly attractive. His manner was amiable, easy-going.

He handed Madeline a metal clipboard. "No probs. Everything's going smooth as silk tonight, but just to make sure I'll go and check the studio."

At the door he was shouldered out of the way by a tall, strongly built man who barged into the room. "Jesus, Madeline!"

Composed, Madeline said, "Carol, do meet our station manager, Gordon Vaughan. Gordon, this is Detective Inspector Ashton."

"We've met, briefly." He gave Carol a perfunctory nod. Vaughan's dark hair was flecked with gray and he had a predatory face, with a hook nose and a heavy jaw. Shoving a sheet of paper at Madeline, he said, "This just came through on my personal fax machine. The guy's obviously a psycho." While Madeline read the fax, Vaughan said to Carol, "The media briefing about Tala was the second item on our six o'clock news." He mouth curled cynically. "I must say you've made an art form out of saying nothing much, Inspector. You'll understand that as a close friend of the Orlando family I'm very interested to know what you really think about her death."

"Perhaps we can discuss it tomorrow, Mr. Vaughan. I'll be calling to make a time to see you, just to clear up a few matters."

"I hope this whole thing can be wrapped up soon,

Inspector. It's very hard on the family and friends."
He switched his attention to Madeline. "Well? What
do you think?"

Madeline was pale, but she said nonchalantly,
"It's not a big deal. He's written to me before."

"Why wasn't I told about it?" Vaughan sounded
aggrieved. "That's why we have security at the
station."

Madeline shrugged. "I asked Carol to have a look
at the letters —"

"We can handle this internally." Vaughan took a
deep breath. "There's no reason to get the police into
the act."

Madeline was matter-of-fact. "Gordon, if I ran to
you every time a would-be fan sent me something
like this I'd spend most of my time in your office."

"Your safety is my responsibility," he said flatly.

"At the least the local police should be advised,"
said Carol. "And it's quite conceivable another media
personality has been his target before. If so, tracing
him might not be difficult."

"Carol, I'd like you to be involved."

Carol tried not to show her impatience. "Madeline,
I've already explained why I can't."

"Perhaps you'll change your mind," said Madeline
as she handed her the fax, "when you know that he
mentions *you*."

CHAPTER TWO

TO: GORDON VAUGHAN

Madeline wasn't there Friday night at seven. You should make her obey you, Gordon. She needs to be punished, don't you agree? I've asked her, over and over, to smile for me, to say, hello, Marquis, I'm thinking of you. That's all, but she won't do it.

If I were you, I'd whip her, a little harder each stroke, to show her who's boss. Or battery acid in her eyes. Her wide open eyes. Then she'd be sorry.

That blonde whore cop can't protect Madeline, no

*matter how often she's with her. Night and day, it
makes no difference.*

*Perhaps I'll get them both in a crowd. They'll
think it's water first, then the burning will start. And
the screaming.*

Marquis

Carol looked up as Mark Bourke came into her
office. She gestured to a chair. "How were your
holidays?"

"Great. Roughing it in the Outback in a four-
wheel drive is the way to go. We went right up to
the very top of Cape York. Forgot all about work and
got a suntan."

"A suntan?" Carol inspected the blistered red of
his nose.

He showed no resentment at her amused tone.
"So Pat got a suntan. I sort of colored up."

"I'm delighted you're feeling fresh and ready to
go. That'll be a help on the Orlando case, which is
turning out to be a headache. I'm being politely
leaned on to hurry up and make up my mind why
she died."

"It boils down to accident or suicide, doesn't it?"

"It's true the mixture of tranquilizers and alcohol
she'd taken would have made her confused and
disoriented, so she could have started the car and
then passed out. I get the impression that's what a
lot of people want to hear."

"You're not considering murder?"

"I'm considering everything." She picked up a
videotape from her in-tray. "I taped the program on
Tala Orlando that went to air on Sunday night. Did
you see it?"

"Nope. We only got back home that afternoon and Pat made me water all the indoor plants and then help with the laundry we'd accumulated." He grinned at Carol. "She's got me so domesticated that I worked until I dropped exhausted into bed."

"It's good for your character," said Carol, thinking that Mark Bourke had been home-oriented even before Pat had married him the year before. He had always been reticent, even with Carol, but she knew he had lived alone for years after his first wife and child died in an accident. She'd called in to his house a couple of times, always on business, and found it almost sterilely neat. Bourke had never socialized much with other cops, but now that he had married Pat James he had been becoming progressively more outgoing.

She slid the videotape into the player but before starting it passed him a copy of the fax that had been sent to Gordon Vaughan the evening before. "Have a look at this before we get to Tala Orlando. It's the most current communication from a stalker Madeline Shipley's been getting stuff from over the last few months. Flowers and then letters before. This is the first fax."

He rubbed his chin as he studied it. "He's canceled the top line giving the originating fax number. Could have been sent from anywhere. The fact he used a typewriter could help, but I wonder why he did. He must know it could be identified where an inkjet or laser printer can't be. Seems pretty well educated — I'm always impressed by people who can use apostrophes." He looked up. "And he has some inside knowledge. He knows you and Madeline Shipley are close friends."

Carol looked at her sergeant sharply, but his blunt, good-natured face was without guile. She said dismissively, "It's not a secret."

As she spoke she thought with irritation of last night. Madeline had insisted they have dinner at her home after she had finished the show, saying she was too tired to go out and that Edna, her housekeeper, had prepared a meal. "Don't you want to be seen with me in a restaurant? Doesn't it fit your image?" Carol had snapped. Ever since Carol had been forced to acknowledge publicly that she was a lesbian, it had seemed to her that Madeline had tried to avoid being seen one-to-one with her.

Madeline denied it, of course, but the idea sat like a stone in Carol's mind and instead of staying the night she had said she was tired and had gone home. She had paid a price for her stand, having vividly erotic dreams, and waking tense and unfulfilled.

She came back to the present as Mark put the copy of the faxed threat back on Carol's desk. "Who's on the investigation?" he asked. "The local cops, or has it been escalated because you were mentioned?"

"Would you believe Tom Brewer?"

"Brewer's handling the investigation?" Bourke raised his eyebrows. "Someone's got a sense of humor."

"Seems that way."

Years ago Tom Brewer had been in the same intake of cadets as Carol, but although they had joined the Police Service together, she had risen steadily up the ranks while his career had stalled. He was a mediocre officer but his real problem had always been his penchant to hit first and ask

14

questions later. Although nothing concrete had ever been proved, internal investigations for brutality and evidence tampering had not helped his career. Brewer himself seemed convinced that there had been some conspiracy to deny him advancement. When Carol was promoted to the rank of inspector, Tom Brewer's resentment had boiled over. He had not only confronted her, accusing her of sleeping her way up the ranks, he had even registered a formal objection, which had been summarily dismissed.

"Have you warned Ms. Shipley that Brewer is heading her way?"

Carol smiled wryly. "Madeline can look after herself."

She punched the remote control of the video machine. As *Tribute to Tala* came up on the screen, she said, "You might have seen the original program that went to air several months ago. It was called, I think, *The Real Tala Orlando* and was so critical of her career and business tactics that she threatened to sue Channel Thirteen and the rest of the network."

Bourke raised a cynical eyebrow. "They seem to have made up. She just recently signed a program deal with them."

When Carol had watched it on Sunday night she had been coldly amused at the skillful way the critical slant of the first program had been changed. Retitled *A Tribute to Tala,* the channel had tacked on a glowing introduction, shots of grieving relatives and associates and an effusive conclusion where the announcer had referred to Tala Orlando as "a flower cut off before her full blossoming."

Watching the screen, Carol said, "We get a full cast of characters in a moment." After the laudatory

15

introduction, Tala Orlando appeared on the screen at one of the media events she had regularly attended.

"To me she always looked brittle enough to break," said Bourke.

Carol agreed. Dressed in her trademark black, anorexically thin, with a gaunt, high-cheekboned face and a narrow mouth, Tala Orlando was shown at a recent media conference where she had announced her television production company's latest coup — the sale of a new quiz show as a concept package to television networks in both Britain and the United States. She didn't mention the embarrassing fact that a previous associate had recently surfaced with claims that the original idea for the quiz show had been his.

Like her body, Tala Orlando's voice lacked weight. She announced her independent company's achievements in a soft, almost colorless monotone, trailing off at the end of sentences as though out of breath.

The screen switched to a series of news shots taken just after her death, most being of friends or relatives as they hurried from cars to the safety of their homes or offices. Bourke grunted as a well-groomed man, good tailoring almost managing to disguise the extra weight he was carrying, emerged from a burgundy Rolls-Royce.

"The broken-hearted husband, Hayden Delray. That isn't the car she died in, surely." Bourke glanced at her.

"It's a twin. They had matching Rollers."

Carol thought Delray was handsome in a fleshy, gone-to-seed way. They watched Delray smooth back his sandy hair as his lawyer fended questions from the swarm of reporters.

"I suppose you know that when Delray married

Tala he conned her into changing Orlando Productions to Orlandel to include his name," Bourke said derisively, "even though she was the one who'd built the company up from nothing."

"If it was fame Delray wanted, it didn't happen, Mark. Tala Orlando was the one who got all the publicity and made all the announcements about the company."

"Well he's getting all the attention now. Hayden Delray can't possibly be his real name."

"It isn't. Apparently he changed it by deed poll in his early twenties."

Bourke grinned at her. "He was John Smith, or something like that. Right?"

"Bruce Schnell, actually."

"Delray's as fake as his new name."

His scorn was so apparent that Carol was interested. "You've met him?"

"No, Pat has." He added sardonically, "Delray likes to be seen at every social event, so Pat's run across him at fund-raisings and openings at the Art Gallery. She says he's a toucher — you know the sort. Can't keep his hands to himself. She swears he'd feel up the Queen if she were visiting."

Carol thought of Bourke's wife with affection. She was a brisk, no-nonsense person with a penetrating laugh and an athletic build. Carol couldn't imagine anyone touching her up without Pat's retaliating, possibly with a well-placed blow.

"Any suggestions Delray is actually playing around?"

This amused Bourke. "Plenty of suggestions he'd *like* to, but the general consensus is that Tala would have his balls if he did."

His attention was drawn back to the television screen. "Here's Tala's sister. She's like a second-rate version, isn't she?"

Robynne Orlando, dressed in an unflattering dark dress featuring flowing panels, was shown being tenderly led to a waiting limousine. Although facially she resembled her more famous sister, her build was heavier and she lacked the look of automatic authority that had been so characteristic of Tala Orlando.

Robynne Orlando's companion was a young woman with masses of curly light hair and an exquisite profile. "Too upset to speak to us," said a faintly resentful voice-over, "Robynne Orlando was comforted by a close personal friend, rising television personality Kimberley Blackland."

Carol smiled to herself. A consummate self-promoter, Kimberley Blackland was a field reporter on Madeline's show. Carol remembered Madeline saying with rueful admiration how Kimberley seized any opportunity to fill in for her during Madeline's rare absences, and how she fought ferociously to have more on-air time than any other reporter. Carol had the cynical thought that the public comforting of Robynne Orlando provided her additional screen time.

"There's the son," said Bourke. "He's from Tala's first marriage, isn't he?"

"Yes. His father died when he was about five."

Looking at the young man's bland, immature face, Carol wondered what he was thinking and feeling. The television camera held him in close-up for some time as the announcer said portentously, "Joshua Orlando, Tala's only son, should inherit a substantial share of his mother's production company. But the question remains, does he have the unique abilities of his mother? The abilities that took Orlandel Productions to the top?"

"I suspect Hayden Delray won't take kindly to the idea of sharing the company with a kid like that," said Bourke.

Having exhausted news shots made in the last few days, the program segued into the original exposé, beginning with a couple of blurry shots of a slightly built man. "Once her brother-in-law, reclusive Nevile Carson accuses Tala Orlando of stealing his concept for the stunning new quiz show, *Take the Risk,* soon to appear on this station, Channel Thirteen," said the voice-over breathlessly. "Could this be a crippling blow to Orlandel Productions if the threatened legal action is taken?"

The scene changed to show Tala Orlando smiling as she accepted an entertainment industry award. The clip included part of her acceptance speech, where she gracefully attributed her success to good luck and the hard work of her staff.

"She's deceptive," said Carol. "In business I gather she was absolutely ruthless."

"Made enemies, of course. Any who'd resent her enough to want her dead?"

"Perhaps, but I'm still not sure whether it was an accident, murder disguised as suicide or she really did kill herself."

"There wasn't a note."

"No, but there was an ambiguous message on her son's answering machine."

Bourke leaned back and put his hands behind his head. "Aren't you tempted to say it's a tragic accident and let the whole thing die down? Even up in the wilds of the Northern Territory Pat and I heard all about it, blow by blow."

Carol didn't return his grin. She indicated a thick blue file on her desk. "Here's the Orlando file. After you've looked at it you can tell me what you think. And you'd better speed-read after we finish watching this program, because I've lined up some interviews for early this afternoon."

Tala Orlando's face gazed imperiously from the screen. The announcer was saying, "With everything to live for, why such a tragic end?" This was followed by a much-repeated shot of the gurney with the sheeted body being trundled to the waiting ambulance. "To die alone in her burgundy Rolls-Royce . . ." the voice continued sorrowfully.

From the moment the news broke that Tala Orlando had been found dead behind the wheel of her luxury car, speculation had boiled. On the surface it could have been suicide. The garage doors were locked, the engine of the Rolls was still idling with impeccable precision, pumping exhaust into the enclosed space. Tala Orlando, immaculately dressed in a black suit, had been slumped over the steering wheel as though overcome before she could activate the electronic garage door opener.

But there were contradictory factors that disturbed Carol. Although the post mortem showed a substantial dose of tranquilizers, apparently she had never been known to take such drugs before; there was no note or prior evidence of depression; there were rumors that her marriage to Hayden Delray was in trouble; lastly, she faced a ferocious battle in court over the rights to her company's new quiz show, *Take the Risk.*

Watching a rare smile on Tala Orlando's pale face as she received congratulations from the Prime Minister for her efforts in earning export dollars for Australia, Carol thought of the police photos of the body, which showed the incongruous cherry-pink skin characteristic of carbon monoxide poisoning. Ironically, Tala had looked far healthier in death than in life.

She said to Bourke, "I've advised the family I'll be releasing the body today. The funeral will be on Friday."

"Do I break out my best dark suit?"

"You do. We'll both attend. It will be an event, of course. Interactions could be interesting."

She froze the action on the screen as the telephone on her desk rang. "Carol Ashton ... Yes. Send him up." Putting down the receiver, she said, "Hayden Delray's here to see me. Says it's urgent."

"What's your take on him?"

Turning off the television, she said, "See what you think of him. I've seen him twice and he's been cooperative. I interviewed him the day after he found the body, and understandably he was shaken. He was upset when I asked him about his marriage, insisting that there had been nothing wrong and they'd been very happy together. In the second interview, I played him the message that his wife left on Joshua Orlando's answering machine, and he was much more together."

When Hayden Delray was shown into Carol's office he gave the prosaic room a cursory glance before his attention settled on Bourke, who had chosen a strategic position near the window. He put out his hand. "We haven't met."

21

Carol introduced them, gestured for Delray to take a seat, and sat down behind her desk. "You said it was urgent?"

He gave a brief, apologetic smile. "Perhaps I exaggerated. It's just with Tala's death . . . Frankly, Inspector, I'll be so relieved when you come to a final decision. I can't believe that Tala killed herself, but equally, I can't believe I've lost her because of some stupid accident . . ." His resonant voice trailed away.

"Why did you want to see me?"

Delray's dark clothing accentuated the red flush of his face and his gut bulged against his discreetly striped shirt as he leaned forward to pass her an opened envelope. "You asked me before whether anything was worrying my wife. Deena, Tala's assistant, found this in her office. Tala had it for days but hadn't mentioned it to me. It must have upset her terribly. Maybe that's why she took the Valium."

Carol checked the envelope, then read the contents. As she handed the letter to Bourke she said to Delray, "It's clearly a preliminary notification from a firm of solicitors of the intention to subpoena Robynne Orlando in the case of Carson versus Orlandel Productions. Would that be particularly disturbing for your wife?"

Delray's face grew redder. "That bastard knew Tala would be distraught if her sister was forced to testify against the company. I suppose you know Carson is Robynne's ex-husband. He's going to claim he came up with the format for *Take the Risk* while they were married, and that she knows Tala stole it from him."

Bourke said, "Surely the fact that your sister-in-law may be testifying against Orlandel wouldn't be enough to drive your wife to take her own life."

Delray swung around in his chair to look at him. "Take her own life? It was an accident. Everyone in the family thinks so. Tala was so upset she didn't know what she was doing." He ran a hand over his face. "I can't believe she's gone."

Carol looked at him reflectively. "We will need to question some of your staff — just routine — and I've made an appointment to see your sister-in-law this afternoon. I presume you've told her about this letter."

"Well, no, I haven't." He took out a handkerchief and blew his nose. "Inspector, you couldn't know the special relationship Tala had with Robynne. After the break-up with Nevile Carson two years ago, Robynne became very depressed, had what I suppose you'd call a nervous breakdown. Tala helped her through, took her into the company, even bought the house next to ours for her. But my wife always worried that Robynne was particularly delicate. Fragile."

"Your sister-in-law said that she had no prescription drugs that your wife could have found and used."

"Did she?" After a moment, he added thoughtfully, "You know, Robynne's always been very highly strung. I mean, if she *did* give Tala some Valium, she might not admit it, even to herself." He rubbed his forehead. "You see what I mean? She might not be able to face the fact that she might be to blame for what happened . . ."

"We get the idea," said Bourke dryly.

23

Delray ignored the comment. "I know you have to question her, Inspector," he said, "but do please remember that Robynne has been shattered by Tala's death." He shook his head. "We all have been."

After he had gone, Bourke said, "He's a phony."

"You wouldn't be influenced by what Pat told you about him, would you?"

Bourke grinned at her. "Of course I would," he said.

CHAPTER THREE

Orlandel Productions was situated in North Sydney near the huge sandstone pylons that supported the soaring gray arch of the Harbour Bridge. "Million-dollar view," said Carol as she gazed over the water to the towers of the city.

Bourke indicated the glistening new building behind them. "To suit a multi-million-dollar company. And counting."

The pale gray letters of *Orlandel Productions* stood out clearly against the polished black marble façade. Glass doors hissed open discreetly. Inside, there was more black marble and a glossy receptionist with perfect teeth and impossibly long red fingernails. "How can I help you?" Her smile was professionally incandescent.

Bourke flashed her a broad smile of his own. "This is Detective Inspector Ashton, and I'm Detective Sergeant Mark Bourke. Has Mr. Delray come back yet?"

The receptionist shook her head regretfully. "I'm so sorry, but he called to say he won't be in today." She brightened. "Is there some other way I can assist you?"

"Why, yes," said Bourke warmly, "there certainly is. While Inspector Ashton speaks with Deena Bush, I'd like to ask you a few questions."

A young man was summoned to take Carol to Deena Bush. She left Bourke leaning companionably against the sleek black counter chatting to the receptionist. Carol saw him laugh as the lift doors closed. She had always admired the way Bourke could disguise the sharpness of his mind with a casual friendliness, gaining information during what seemed to be the most relaxed and ordinary of conversations.

"Deena's in Ms. Orlando's office," said the awkward young man who had come to fetch Carol. He led her along a thickly carpeted corridor. "Like, she's wondering what's going to happen to her," he confided. "Now that her boss's gone, like."

"You mean Deena won't have a job?"

The young man blinked at her. "Like, I don't even know if *my* job's safe." His prominent Adam's apple bobbed as he swallowed. "See, Mr. Delray says there's going to be big changes, now that he's taking over." He stuck his head around a half-open door that had Tala Orlando's name in gold letters. "Deena? Someone to see you."

Deena Bush, Tala Orlando's personal assistant, was a nervous young woman with bad skin and long, lank semi-blonde hair. After Carol introduced herself, Deena reluctantly sat down, twining her skinny legs around each other and sitting poised on the edge of the chair, as though anxious to get away. "I don't know anything," she said. "Really I don't."

"Just routine," said Carol soothingly. "I know you've signed a statement, but I just want to go over a few things."

As she spoke she glanced around Tala Orlando's luxurious office, which had the prime position at the corner of the building that gave a captivating view of the bridge and harbor. Carol was surprised at how feminine the office was. She had expected a slick, functional room, in tune with Tala Orlando's brisk persona. The soft lines and pastel colors surprised her. On the walls, instead of the anticipated stills from Orlandel's catalog of successful series, there were delicate watercolors of rural scenes.

She leaned forward on the cream and rose striped chair and said pleasantly, "All this must have been a shock for you."

Her sympathy elicited an immediate response. "Oh, it has been! It's been dreadful!"

Carol indicated the piles of documents that covered the top of the cream-colored desk. "You've been going through Ms. Orlando's papers?"

Deena looped her scraggly hair behind her ears. "Well, it's like this, you see. Mr. Delray's moving in here. As soon as possible, he says." Her resentment was plain. "And I have to sort everything out for

27

him." Her mouth turned down. "I don't know how I'm supposed to decide what he wants and what he doesn't want."

"Mr. Delray told me this morning that you found a particular envelope and gave it to him."

Deena looked at her warily. "Yeah. It was in the back of the top drawer of the desk." She shrugged. "Looked like it might be important."

Carol said pleasantly, "Did you read it?"

"Well, I had to, didn't I?" Deena was defensive. "I mean, how would I know it was important if I didn't?"

"So you knew about the court case."

"Well, not that much." Deena bit her lip. "I mean, just what everybody else knows. Nothing special."

"You were at Ms. Orlando's house the night before she died."

Deena twitched. "Just for a while. To have some urgent papers signed," she said rapidly. "I wasn't there for the dinner. I left really early."

"You didn't notice anything unusual?"

She shook her head hard. "No. Nothing. I just got the papers signed and I left."

Although Carol was accustomed to nervousness in perfectly innocent people when they were questioned by the police, she was interested in the level of tension Deena Bush was showing. "Ms. Orlando called you here, in the office, the next morning. You were the last person she phoned before she died."

"I *know*." Deena put her hand to her mouth. "I can't stop thinking about that. It's *awful*."

"Tell me about the conversation."

"She sounded the same as always. Asked me to

cancel some appointments she had that afternoon. Said that she'd reschedule them later." She added with a hint of defiance, "And I can't tell you anything else." She looked around the room. "I've got to get back to work."

Carol gave her a companionable smile. "You say Mr. Delray's moving in, but it doesn't seem much like a man's office, does it?"

"Oh, it's not going to stay like this." She gestured with both hands. "It's so pretty, and Tala loved it like this, but Mr. Delray's having everything taken out." Her voice rang with indignation. "He's going to refurnish it completely."

Carol inclined her head toward the stunning view. "I can see why he would want to change offices."

"That isn't why," Deena said spitefully. "He just wants anything about his wife out of the building. You know, like she never was here at all."

Back in the car, Bourke said, "That was interesting. I begged a cup of coffee from Tiffany on the reception desk, so she got someone to take me through the offices to the kitchen. I started chatting to a few people, and it seems Hayden Delray is putting his grief aside to seize the helm of the company and steer it the way he wants it to go."

"I got the same message. Big changes and a lot of unsettled staff. And Delray is moving into his wife's office after he obliterates anything that reminds him of her. Deena Bush seems worried that as soon as she finishes sorting through Tala's papers she could be out of a job."

"I got the feeling there was a fierce loyalty for Tala. She drove her staff hard, but did the same to herself. Her husband, however, has never been all that popular." Bourke turned off the freeway at the Northbridge sign. "Nothing specific was said, but the general opinion seems to be that he's all sizzle and no sausage."

Northbridge was an older suburb with some apartment buildings but mainly free-standing houses that grew in size and importance as Bourke drove along Sailors Bay Road toward the prized harbor view enclaves.

He continued, "Everyone I spoke to seems to be pretty much in a state of shock over her death, that's probably why they were so forthcoming. I casually dropped the idea of suicide into the conversation, and got a no way from everyone. Just before she died Tala had green-lighted a new series on technology that she was sure was going to be a hit, and she'd been planning an overseas promotional trip for next month."

"Did you have a chance to ask about Tala Orlando's son?"

"The consensus is he's been spoiled rotten in the past, but his mother was in the process of lowering the boom. She'd bankrolled him for his studies and he had to come up with the results, or get a paying job and support himself."

"What was Joshua's reaction to this ultimatum?"

Bourke grinned. "I gather he made all the right noises. I would have done the same — it's clear that Tala was more than formidable when she was angry."

Carol pointed. "Second left here." As Bourke

30

turned into the quiet, leafy street, she said, "And what about Robynne Orlando?"

"Tala gave her sister some sort of job in the company with a title like Publicity Liaison, or something like that, but she doesn't seem to actually *do* much."

"On the right, Mark. The house with the sandstone pillars, at the top of the drive." As they got out of the car, she said, "Robynne owed a lot to her sister — a house, a job. I wonder if her brother-in-law will continue to be so generous."

Robynne Orlando's house sat with its back to the road, its face set to the east and the beguiling conjunction of land and water that made its resale value so high. "Which was Tala's house?" asked Bourke as they got out of the car.

Carol indicated the imposing house to their left. "It's larger than this one, but it has the same Middle Harbour views. From the street you can see the doors of the double garage where she was found."

As they walked down the drive to Robynne Orlando's house, Mark pointed to a green gate in the stone wall that separated the sisters' houses. "Is it locked?"

"No. Tala had it put in so she and her sister were saved the effort of walking up to the street when they wanted to visit."

"Perhaps it was used for assignations," said Bourke. "There was one other thing I gleaned in my conversations at Orlandel — a merest hint that *Tala* was the one who was having an affair, not Hayden."

Robynne Orlando opened the door to them. Carol found herself agreeing with the assessment Mark Bourke had given while watching the program that morning. She was a blurred version of her famous sister. Where Tala Orlando had been taut, sharp, autocratic, Robynne Orlando seemed limited, ineffectual. They had the same dark hair, high cheekbones and narrow mouth, but there was no command in Robynne Orlando's manner. In only one way was she more impressive than her sister — her voice was deeper and had more expression.

"I don't know why you need to see me again, Inspector Ashton. I've told you everything I know."

She led them through the house to a room at the back and waved them to seats. "Why don't you just go ahead and admit my sister killed herself?" She wiped her eyes with a lace handkerchief. Her face was swollen and her skin blotchy. "Why do you want to torture the family this way?"

Surprised that she wasn't toeing the family line, Carol said, "So you think it was suicide? Not an accident? But you described your sister's behavior the night before as being quite normal."

Robynne Orlando twisted the damp handkerchief between her fingers. "Suicide," she said. Fresh tears ran down her cheeks. "Or worse." She shielded her eyes with one hand.

Bourke opened his mouth to ask a question, but Carol shook her head slightly. She wanted to let silence encourage the woman to talk. She glanced around Robynne Orlando's spacious living room, which was flooded with light from huge picture windows overlooking a stone patio. When Tala Orlando had bought her sister this house she had apparently spared no expense, from the extensive gardens to the imposing façade. The austere black and white entrance hall had been softened by an interior fountain surrounded by greenery under a huge skylight, but this room seemed to have been the work of a decorator who believed in making stark statements. There were no curtains to soften the wall of tinted glass, and the expanse of buff carpet was broken only by a few emaciated pieces of furniture. Carol and Bourke had been seated on an angular leather and metal couch that was as uncomfortable as it looked, and Robynne Orlando had sunk into a matching chair separated from them by a black metal and glass coffee table bearing a single blood-red silk rose in a tall obsidian vase.

Robynne blew her nose. "I don't suppose you want to even consider that someone helped Tala die." She glared at them through swollen, reddened eyes. "I know my sister better than anyone. Tala never took *any* drugs, particularly not tranquilizers. Believe me, she hardly touched alcohol because she said it made her fuzzy. She hated not to be in complete control."

"Her blood profile showed diazepam — Valium." Carol's tone was neutral.

"I've no idea where she got it." Robynne searched for a dry section in her handkerchief. "Those days before she died — she was uptight, tense. Maybe, just that once, she used something to calm her down." She hiccupped a sob.

"You don't have any tranquilizers that she could have taken without you knowing?"

"Absolutely not, Inspector!"

After a pause, Carol said, "You said suicide — or worse. What did you mean?"

"Did I? I'm not sure what I meant."

"Murder?" said Bourke helpfully.

The word seemed to stun Robynne Orlando. "Murder?" she repeated faintly. "You think someone killed Tala?"

Carol exchanged glances with Bourke. She was beginning to suspect that Tala's sister had been manipulating the conversation in this direction from the beginning. "Do you have any information that might indicate she was murdered?"

"No, of course not. I would have told you." She gripped her clasped hands tight against her chest. "It's just that I can't believe that she would kill herself, by accident or on purpose. I can't believe it."

"This must be a dreadful time for you," said Bourke sympathetically, "but we have to ask these questions. Can you think of anyone who would want to harm your sister?"

"She had enemies. Everyone very successful has enemies."

Bourke smiled gently at her. "Were there problems in her marriage?"

She turned her head sharply toward him. "Problems? Who told you that? Hayden and Tala were very happy together. I would have known if there was anything wrong. We weren't just sisters — we were best friends. There were no secrets between us."

"But she didn't tell you that your ex-husband intends to subpoena you as a witness in the court case he's bringing against Orlandel Productions."

Robynne dropped her hands into her lap. "Hayden called this afternoon and told me so, but I don't believe him. Even Nevile wouldn't do that to me. He couldn't."

Agitated, she heaved herself out of the chair. "Tala would never let it happen to me!"

"Aunt Robynne . . ." said a voice at the door.

"Josh! Did you hear? They're going to make me go to court!"

Carol looked closely at Joshua Orlando as he coaxed his aunt back into her chair. She knew Tala Orlando's son had just turned twenty-one, but he looked younger. Presumably Joshua took after his father; there was little resemblance to his mother in his face or bearing. He was short and squarely built, with straight brown hair, pale blue eyes and spongy, unformed features. Carol thought he probably did body building, as his neck and shoulders were thick and his chest bulged with muscles under his white T-shirt.

Carol introduced Mark Bourke, then said, "Mr. Orlando, since you're here, I have a couple of questions for you, if you don't mind."

He nodded affably. "Sure. Anything to help."

Carol stood. "While Sergeant Bourke finishes here, perhaps we could go to another room . . ."

"Josh, you don't have to answer questions, you know." Robynne Orlando's tone was surprisingly sharp.

"Hey, I don't mind." He nodded to Carol. "Let's go out on the patio."

The patio, edged with a stone balustrade, overlooked the steep fall to the solid blue of deep water. Carol could see the roof of a boathouse below. There was an uninterrupted view of Middle Harbour

35

all the way to the Spit Bridge she crossed every day. From this distance it was a toy structure with tiny cars streaming across it.

When they were settled in heavy white metal chairs, Joshua Orlando smiled at her engagingly. "Aunt Robynne still thinks of me as a little kid. Even so, I think she's glad to have me staying with her for a few days." He became grave. "So what do you want to know?"

"You inherit one-third of your mother's estate." She didn't mention the recent codicil to the will that delayed his inheritance until he was thirty.

He nodded agreeably. "Yes, that's right. And Hayden gets a third and so does Aunt Robynne. It's very fair."

And will make you all very rich. Aloud, she said, "Had your mother discussed the terms of her will with you?"

His shrug was rather too casual. "Only in a general way. It was all academic, of course. No one had any idea that this accident would happen."

Carol leaned back in the chair, enjoying the late autumn sunshine. "You're not concerned about the special provision that applies to you?"

"Provision? You mean the condition I have to wait until I'm thirty? My mother was angry with me over something. She would have changed it."

"She died before she could."

Joshua didn't seem affronted by Carol's blunt statement. "It's no big deal," he said. "If I need money, I can borrow against my inheritance. And Aunt Robynne would always make sure I was okay."

"Your mother carried life insurance." Although

she already had full details of the policy, she was interested to know how much Tala's son knew.

"Of course she was insured — for a million, actually — because she *was* the company. That's why the whole sum will go to Orlandel Productions." He gave her a small, shrewd smile. "But of course you know all about that, don't you? The fact that there's no suicide waiver, so it doesn't matter how she died."

Carol felt repelled by his manner — he seemed to be indifferent to the fact that his mother had been dead only a few days. Reminding herself that he could just be acting tough, she said, "Your mother's loss must be a blow to the company. Will you be involved in Orlandel Productions in the future?"

He gave an incredulous laugh. "Involved? Why would I be? I'm at university doing a degree in economics. I've never had the slightest interest in my mother's company. Besides, Hayden wouldn't accept any input from me, now that he's got it all to himself."

Carol was intrigued by the thread of resentment under his words. She said innocently, "I suppose the loss of your mother will be felt very keenly by the company."

"She made the company, and she ran the company." He bit off the words.

"Certainly your mother was very much to the forefront as far as publicity was concerned, but I was under the impression that the company was run as an equal partnership between your mother and your stepfather."

Joshua gave a bitter laugh. "He tell you that? He'd be nothing without my mother. You watch

Orlandel fall through the floor, now that he's got hold of it."

Carol didn't speak until he shifted uneasily and cleared his throat. She said, "How do you get on with your stepfather?"

"Well enough." His face was blank.

"The message your mother left on your answering machine seemed to suggest something else."

"You may think so, Inspector. *I* don't." There was a hint of insolence in his manner. "My mother wasn't thinking straight. After all, she accidentally killed herself only a few hours later."

"I hope you don't mind too much, but I'd like you to listen to the message again." Carol took a microcassette recorder from her briefcase.

He sat back and folded his arms. "I don't mind."

Carol watched him as Tala's soft, wispy voice began. *Josh. I wish you were home. This is very difficult for me, but I can't ignore what's happened. Hayden told me what you said. It's just impossible to go on like this. I have to do something. There was a pause, then she repeated more faintly, I have to do something.*

Clicking off the recorder, Carol said, "When I saw you before, you said you had no idea what your mother thought you had said to your stepfather."

"I still don't. He and I often disagree. Just a clash of personalities, nothing else." He leaned forward persuasively. "Look, Inspector, my mother wasn't herself when she left that message. I mean, she was accustomed to Hayden and me arguing over something. It was nothing unusual."

"What do you think she meant when she said she had to do something?"

"Frankly, I've got no idea. My mother was upset. She wasn't making sense."

Carol remembered that when she had questioned Hayden Delray he too had described the relationship with his stepson as "a clash of personalities" and had commented that his wife's last message "didn't make any sense."

"Have you discussed this recording with Mr. Delray?" she asked mildly.

Joshua sat up. "What, rehearsed our answers, you mean?" He seemed sourly amused, rather than offended. "Hey, Inspector, you're putting way too much importance on this, you know. It was an accident. It's awful, but that's the way it is."

I'm beginning to doubt it, Carol thought.

Before she could frame another question, Bourke came out of the house holding his mobile phone. Handing it to her, he said, "I'm sorry to interrupt, but there's an urgent call for you."

Madeline's voice was unsteady. "Carol, forgive me. I asked them to track you down."

"What's happened? Are you all right?"

"I'm fine. It's my car. Someone's poured acid into it. The seats, everywhere. And there's a note . . ."

CHAPTER FOUR

You've made me do this, Madeline. I tried to get your attention, but you won't do what I want you to do.

I'd like you to think about this: what if it had been your body, not just the inside of your car? Your beautiful skin bubbling and peeling. Pulling away from your flesh in strips.

I have your attention now.

I see you every day, Madeline. Don't make me angry again.

Marquis

The corner of Channel Thirteen's executive car park had attracted a buzz of attention. People who had come out of the building were held back by yellow tape, watching crime scene technicians examine the dark green BMW that stood with all its doors open.

"It's pretty much a write-off," said Madeline to Carol. She was obviously making an effort to be nonchalant but looked white and shaken. "The insurance company will scream blue murder — the whole interior will have to be replaced." With an attempt at humor, she added, "And I'll have to explain it's an act of Marquis. Do you think they'll buy that?"

"The note was in an envelope under the driver's windscreen wiper."

"That's right. I suppose I should have left it there, but I read it." Madeline drew a shaky breath. "Why's he doing this? Because he hates me?"

A technician wearing protective clothing and goggles was leaning into the front compartment of the BMW collecting samples of ruined upholstery. When Carol moved forward to peer over his shoulder, blinking at the fumes that stung her eyes, he straightened. "Don't breathe this stuff in, Inspector."

"Any idea what was used?"

"I can guess. Analysis will tell us for sure, but I'm betting it's basically sodium hydroxide, better known as caustic soda. Very nasty, and highly corrosive."

"And easy to obtain."

"Sure. Caustic soda's found in oven cleaners, drain unblockers, some paint strippers. You can get it in any supermarket."

Carol turned to the short, stout woman who headed the unit. "Liz, treat this as very urgent. I'd like a full report as soon as possible."

"I'm sure you would," said Liz sarcastically. She shoved her wire-rimmed spectacles back into position and grinned at Carol. "But since it's *you* asking, you've got it."

Madeline looked up at Carol as they walked back into the TV station. "Another Carol Ashton conquest. Like me, that woman's captivated by you."

Carol's concern about what had happened to the BMW made a playful reply impossible. "Madeline, this is getting serious. A physical attack on something belonging to you is very significant, especially when it's accompanied by a written threat. I want you to take some fairly rigorous precautions until we get this guy."

Jim Borlie came out of Madeline's office. "Are you okay? I've just heard. It's terrible."

Watching his soft, concerned face, Carol thought, The note said, I see you every day.

"I'm fine, Jim," said Madeline cheerfully. "Would you mind going to the canteen and getting me a pot of fresh coffee? And biscuits, or something like that." As he hurried off, her expression changed as she sank onto a chair. "I need a caffeine jolt, darling, and you probably could do with one too." She sighed. "It's stupid, I know, but I feel absolutely exhausted. This guy's getting to me."

"When did you park your car?"

"This morning, early." A trace of a wicked smile curved her mouth. "I didn't sleep well. Might have something to do with the fact you ran out on me last night."

42

"How early?"

"About eight, I think. I used my card to get in, parked in my marked spot and went inside. I didn't see the car again until this afternoon. I had an appointment in the city, so it was about three o'clock when I discovered what had happened. It totally freaked me out, so after I told security, I called you."

"Was the BMW locked?"

Madeline made a face. "I never lock it in the car park here. Don't lecture me. No one could steal it because they wouldn't be able to get out without a plastic card."

"You have a touching faith in boom gates," said Carol dryly. "And one that's totally unjustified, in fact —" She broke off as Borlie came through the door with a tray.

As he set it down he said to Madeline, "Kimberley wondered if you were okay to go on tonight." His voice was quite neutral.

"God!" Madeline laughed, energized. "That woman just never gives up! Tell Kimberley I appreciate her concern, but there's no problem. Everything tonight will be as usual." Still smiling, she said to Carol, "Have to watch that one. She might slip something into my coffee, just to get on air!"

When Carol got back to her office she found Bourke waiting for her. He put down the coroner's report on Tala Orlando that he'd been reading. "Bad as it sounded? I hate it when a car gets hurt."

Ignoring his levity, she passed him the text of the Marquis's note she'd jotted down before the crime unit had taken it for testing. "Things are escalating. First occasional flowers with a note, then letters, now this attack on her car."

"Think she'll be next?"

Carol spread her hands. "It's always hard to say what someone like this will do. I've asked Madeline to be very careful. I suggested she move out of her house, but she refused. She says she's okay because she has a housekeeper living there full time."

"A housekeeper with a degree in karate? Otherwise that mightn't be much help."

Carol smiled reluctantly when she thought of Edna, a little tough-talking woman who had a ramrod back and a snappy manner. "Edna's pretty formidable, in her own way."

"Speaking of formidable, the Super wants to see you."

"It's about the interim Orlando report, of course. I left it on his desk yesterday, and I don't think it said what he wanted to hear." Superintendent Edgar was usually content to use a minimum of supervision over competent officers, but Carol had found him uncharacteristically intrusive over the Orlando case.

"I was notably conscientious and read the copy you left me." Bourke gave a mock salute with a folder. "I agree with you. There isn't enough evidence to make a decision one way or the other at the moment. It would help to know where Tala Orlando got the diazepam that was found in her blood, since she apparently never took tranquilizers and there wasn't even an empty prescription bottle in the house. And why was she drinking champagne in the mid-morning, apparently by herself?" He grinned at her. "And I wonder why there were so few finger-

44

prints in the car. I mean, *I'd* keep a Rolls-Royce spotless too, but I doubt if I'd wipe the controls clear of fingerprints every time I used it."

"We have to find out where she got the Valium."

"After you left the room this morning with Joshua Orlando, I went back to the subject of tranquilizers and asked Robynne whether she'd ever been prescribed them in the past. She told me it was years ago and she'd thrown out the remaining pills. What was interesting was that the question made her *very* uptight. Makes me wonder if her charming brother-in-law didn't have something when he hinted strongly that she might have contributed to her sister's death."

Carol frowned. "You know, Mark, she shares the same house cleaner as her sister. I want you to re-interview Isabel Snipes-More and see what she's noticed around Robynne's house in the line of prescription drugs or any bottles of pills."

"Isabel Snipes-More?" said Bourke, clearly delighted. "Does she look like her name?"

Carol's lips twitched. "You'll find out when you meet her. She was at Tala Orlando's house the morning she died and, as far as we know, she was the last person to see her alive."

As the phone on her desk burred, Carol sighed and snatched up the receiver before it could ring again. When she hung up she said, "Tom Brewer's coming over to report on the Marquis letters. Once he's done the preliminary work, I'd like us to take it over."

"Isn't your plate pretty full with Tala Orlando? Sure you want something else to worry about?"

"This is personal, Mark."

Bourke ran his hand over the stubble on his

head — apparently he thought that the fact he was balding could be disguised by a super-short haircut. He didn't say anything, but it was clear that he was uncomfortable with her decision.

Unreasonably annoyed, she said, "And don't forget that *I'm* mentioned in one letter."

"Do you really think you're a target? The mention of a blonde cop could have been to impress upon her how much he knew. Nothing more."

"Mark —" She broke off as Tom Brewer strolled through the door without knocking.

"Long time no see, Inspector." He put an ironic emphasis on her title. He nodded to Bourke. "Hey, Mark."

Carol kept her expression neutral. Brewer was whippet-thin, with a loose-limbed, nonchalant walk and untidy, faintly grubby clothes. Seeing him after such a long interval, Carol was again struck by how much she disliked little things about him — the way he chewed gum constantly, his bitten fingernails, his brash stare.

"Have you completed your report?" she said crisply.

He shook his head. "Nah. But I've got some info for you." Chewing steadily, he slid into a chair and opened a notebook. "Want to hear it?"

"Please," she snapped.

Carol heard Bourke's soft laugh. She shot him a cold look. *He* might be amused by Brewer. She wasn't.

Then she thought, *Where the hell is my sense of humor? I should be able to laugh at this.*

After much flipping of pages, Brewer had located the notes he wanted. "First, the bread and butter stuff. We've got one fax, source unknown, and ten letters posted over the last two months. Shipley's assistant had the brains to keep the envelopes, so we know they were dropped into post boxes all over Sydney. Doesn't seem to be any pattern there. Paper is high quality white bond, mass produced, so no joy there either. No prints of any use." He shifted his gum to his other cheek. "Better luck with the typewriter. If we find it, we can make a positive ID. The document guys say it's almost certainly a Brother electric portable with a correcting tape. When he makes mistakes he always fixes them up by overtyping with the white tape, then switching back to the black carbon ribbon. He makes typos, but that's because he's probably a two-finger typist, not because he can't spell." He grinned at Carol. "Unlike me. Can't spell at all. Never could."

"I'm assuming English is his native language."

Brewer referred to his notebook. "Seems to be. And his vocabulary is good, his grammar's okay and he knows how to punctuate." He grinned again. "Like I said, unlike me."

Bourke said, "Have you had time to get a psychological profile?"

"Don't believe in them. Lot of claptrap." Brewer scratched his nose. "But I knew the inspector would want one, so of course I did." He paused and tilted his head, looking interrogatively at Carol.

"Congratulations," she said dryly.

He gave a snort of laughter, then shuffled through the pages of his dog-eared notebook. "Let's see now . . . the psychologist says our perp is probably male, although a woman isn't entirely out of the question, and, like I said before, well-educated. Age?

47

Well that's a bit dicey. It's just a guess that he's mid-twenties to mid-thirties . . . Maybe. Almost certainly working alone. Nothing much to be got from the name he's using. A marquis is a rank in European nobility and he may have chosen it because he fancies himself a new Marquis de Sade. Or the word may have some personal significance for him alone. What else? He's obsessive-compulsive, probably has some history of sadistic sexual behavior and —"

He squinted at his notes. "Has a narcissistic personality disorder. That's a fancy way of saying he's up himself. He thinks he's smarter than all of us put together."

"There's been a physical attack on Madeline Shipley's car today," Carol said. "Corrosive fluid throughout the interior while it was parked at Channel Thirteen. There was a note signed Marquis. I'd like you to pick up a copy from the lab."

"Well," said Brewer, pleased. "This makes things much more interesting. I'd say Shipley better watch out. He'll attack her himself, next time."

"Did the psychologist suggest that was a possibility?"

Brewer chuckled at Carol's question. "Nah. That's my take on it. And I think I'm a hundred-bloody-percent right." He snapped his notebook shut.

"When can I expect your written report?" asked Carol.

"Give me a go," he protested. He got to his feet. "But I can see it's urgent, so I'll get going on it." With an ironic half-salute, he was gone.

Carol smiled unwillingly when Bourke threw up his hands and pulled a face. "Yes," she said, "I was tempted to thump him too."

Superintendent Edgar's office was larger than Carol's but featured the same anonymous beige walls and standard-issue furniture. The man himself was silver-haired, smooth, personable, with an agreeable, rather self-satisfied manner.

"Carol, I don't want you to feel I'm pressuring you." He tapped the tips of his steepled fingers together. "But as you've now released Tala Orlando's body, I'm wondering if that means you're near the end of your inquiries?"

"I'm afraid not. There are a lot of loose ends." She watched him frown. "For example, I haven't been able to interview Nevile Carson yet because he's been out of Sydney. His legal action is against the company, not Ms. Orlando herself, but all the accusations that his idea was stolen have been directed at her." She indicated the red folder in front of him. "I put details in the interim report you have."

"Have you formed an opinion about her death? Are there likely to be any charges?"

Carol hid her cynical amusement. Superintendent Edgar was a consummate player of departmental politics, always allying himself with those who could help his advancement. From the time Carol had been given the case her superior's unusual interest in her day-to-day investigations had indicated considerable pressure coming from somewhere.

She said, "It is in my report . . ."

"Yes, yes, I've read it." He flicked at the red cover but didn't open it. "So what you're saying is that it's still up in the air. Orlando's death could have been an accident, or suicide?"

"Or murder." Carol again indicated the report. "I've briefly outlined the possibility that it might be set up."

The superintendent looked displeased. "Surely that's not likely."

"I am working to clear it up as soon as possible."

"Of course." He cleared his throat. "The commissioner hasn't spoken to you?"

"No, he hasn't." They both knew his question was designed to indicate to Carol that concern about the case went to the very top. She wondered if it were true. Throughout Carol's career the commissioner had been her mentor, always taking a personal interest in her progress. He had often spoken to her directly about high-profile cases she had been given, but on the subject of Tala Orlando she'd heard nothing from him.

Superintendent Edgar shoved his chair away from his desk. The interview was clearly over. "Well, Carol, I'm sure I can rely on you . . ." Unspoken was *to do the right thing.*

Carol knew the script. "You can," she said.

Carol left work late enough to miss the evening

peak-hour traffic. Madeline was attending a charity cocktail party after she finished her program, so Carol was going home. Driving on automatic pilot, she found herself swooping down the curves of Spit Road toward the bridge across Middle Harbour. It was dark, and the lit ribbon of roadway soared across the dark water. In daylight this view always soothed her — the steep fall of the land meeting the deep blue of the harbor, seagulls gliding, white yachts tethered and swinging in the tide. Even when she was in a hurry Carol rarely shared the impatience of other motorists halted because the Spit Bridge had opened to let craft through. She loved to be one of the first cars in the column of frozen traffic, watching the huge section of bridge swing up, light glancing through the heavy steel mesh as the masts paraded through in stately procession.

As she crossed the bridge she decided to leave the main road and take the less direct but quieter way home, so she turned left and zoomed up the winding route. She was forced to brake hard as a brush-tailed possum ran onto the road. It stopped in the middle, mesmerized by her headlights.

There was no other traffic, so she sat patiently while it dithered about what it wanted to do. Because most nights she fed apples and bananas to possums that came down from the eucalyptus gums overhanging the long wooden deck that ran the length of her house, she was familiar with their inclination to run blindly about if panicked.

After sitting for a moment she laughed, put on her hazard lights and undid her seat belt. This one certainly wasn't decisive. As she shooed it out of the way she suddenly thought of how Sybil had spent weeks coaxing a wary mother possum and her baby to take food from her hand. Carol was startled by the shaft of grief she felt. What was Sybil doing at this moment? Talking? Laughing? But of course it was early morning in Britain. Sybil would be waking up, half a world away.

The possum scuttled safely up a tree and Carol got back into her car. She flicked off the hazard lights and put it into gear. *I could call her, as soon as I get home.*

Jeffrey and Sinker were waiting under the porch light, each bursting with feline indignation at her tardiness. As she opened the front door they whipped past her and vanished in the direction of the kitchen with sharp cries of outrage.

"Okay, cats. I'm on my way." Her voice sounded loud in the dark hallway. Usually Carol didn't mind spending time alone, but tonight the emptiness of the house depressed her. She turned on every light on her way to join the cats at their station by the refrigerator.

The phone rang, shrill in the quiet house. Carol's heart leapt. *Sybil? Perhaps she's calling to say she's coming home.*

"I can get away from this cocktail party early, if you like." It was Madeline's slightly husky voice. "In fact, I could come over, right now."

Carol felt an anticipatory tightening, but she said quickly, "I'm really tired . . ."

"Tomorrow night? Are you going to be really tired tomorrow night?"

"Maybe not. I'll call you."

"Please." Madeline laughed softly. "I'm dying for love of you."

Carol had just put down the receiver when the phone rang again. Sybil? It would be ironic if she were to call straight after Madeline.

"Carol? Where have you been? You're home late, as usual."

"Aunt Sarah. How are you?" Carol felt let down that it wasn't Sybil, yet perversely relieved at the same time.

"I'm always well, dear. I need a favor."

"For my favorite aunt — anything."

"As I keep pointing out, I'm your *only* aunt, Carol. I don't suppose you've noticed, but there's a big rally in Sydney on Saturday against nuclear testing in the Pacific. Of course, I could go back to the Blue Mountains afterwards, but I thought I'd stay with you for the weekend, if that's okay, or maybe a few days longer. Besides, if I get arrested, you can bail me out."

Carol found herself smiling. Her Aunt Sarah both exasperated and amused her, but Carol adored her, probably because she was the only person with whom Carol felt totally safe. "You've got a front door key, Aunt Sarah. Come down any time, and if I'm not here, let yourself in."

"You can't work twenty-four hours a day." Aunt Sarah was brusque. "I expect you to spend some time with me. You're entirely too solitary these days."

"Don't bully me, Aunt, or I won't look forward to seeing you."

After she had broken the connection Carol stood

looking pensively out onto the darkened deck. Jeffrey, Sybil's cat, twined around her legs, crying starvation. Carol swept his ginger body into her arms and squeezed him. *I could call her right now.* Jeffrey squawked and she put him down. *But I won't. It would make it worse for both of us.*

CHAPTER FIVE

During her early morning run through paths in the bush reserve at Seaforth Oval, Carol thought about Madeline's stalker. He had access to both a fax machine and a typewriter. The fax could have been sent from anywhere, but if they found the typewriter it could be identified positively. But first, they needed a suspect.

Carol called to Olga, her neighbor's German shepherd, who always ran with her in the morning. Olga had dashed off into thick undergrowth after some fascinating scent and Carol jogged in place while she waited. She was at the top of a cliff that dropped sheer to the water below. The sun was just rising and the first rays dazzled her as they reflected back from the office towers in far distant Chatswood. Next the light struck windows of houses nestled in prized positions in bushland around the calm gray-blue of Middle Harbour, casting strange square patches of light onto the still water.

This beauty usually soothed her, but today she was angry and frustrated. She had no idea who Madeline's stalker was, but his faceless malice was frightening. It could be someone that Madeline spoke to every day, someone secretly laughing behind the mask of a concerned face. Or he could be a total stranger, who listened and watched and followed. It would help to limit any possibles to Madeline's television station, but a preliminary check of the security at Channel Thirteen showed that anyone determined could get in unchallenged.

"Olga! Come here!" There was a commotion in the bush and Olga, looking pleased with herself, shot out. Resuming her run, Carol considered what Marquis had said about Madeline and herself. *That blonde whore cop can't protect Madeline, no matter how often she's with her. Night and day, it makes no difference.* Did that indicate he knew either of them well? Was the mention of day and night a snide reference to the depth of their relationship?

Carol's thoughts skittered away. What depth of relationship *did* she have with Madeline? Carol wasn't even sure what she felt for her. Madeline was ... Madeline. How could she sum her up? Magnetically attractive, implacably ambitious, successful in the ruthless world of television, firmly in the closet and unlikely to open the door voluntarily.

The anger Carol felt about the damage to the BMW had been in part because Madeline had been so shaken and uncharacteristically vulnerable. But was that an indication of the depth of her feelings toward Madeline, or just the operation of primal fear at the threat of a concealed and malevolent enemy? Carol found herself agreeing with Tom Brewer over one thing — the next attempt was likely to be on Madeline herself.

Carol had sent Mark Bourke to interview the house cleaner again, and then see Ruby and Rex Courtold, a married couple who, with Madeline, Gordon Vaughan and Robynne Orlando, had been guests at the dinner party the night before Tala died. She herself had an interview with Nevile Carson, who had flown into Sydney that morning.

Nevile Carson's apartment was on the top floor of a discreetly luxurious building strategically placed high on the slopes above Balmoral Beach. As he ushered her through his front door, Carol's eyes were irresistibly drawn to the sweep of the breath-taking view, which stretched from the crescent of Balmoral Beach below across blue-green water to the serrated sandstone headlands guarding the entrance to Sydney Harbour. Carol stared through them at the line of the horizon, imagining the vast span of the Pacific Ocean running thousands of miles to the South American coast.

"This is beautiful," she said.

He nodded. "It is." He gestured toward the

majestic bulk of the Manly ferry gliding from right to left as though programmed to add a little extra to the scene. "And there's always something happening."

As she sat down, Carol appraised Robynne Orlando's ex-husband. Neatly dressed in beige pants and a plain tan pullover, he was lightly built, with long thin hands. His narrow face was unremarkable, his pale eyes blinking behind tortoise-shell glasses and his thin brown hair combed carefully forward. Although his appearance was average to the point of anonymity, his voice was a surprisingly resonant bass. "I'm sorry I couldn't see you before this, Inspector Ashton, but I've been tied up with business, mostly interstate." He seated himself opposite her and linked his bony fingers. "You want to see me about the case I have pending against Orlandel, I presume."

"That and other things, Mr. Carson." She paused, waiting to see what he would say to fill the silence. Most people would feel compelled to say something, but he sat completely still and watched her.

Finally she said, "Please tell me about the last time you saw Tala Orlando. I'm interested in anything, including your impressions of her state of mind."

"Open-ended questions, Inspector?" He smiled slightly. "By far the best kind."

"I find out more that way," she said, deliberately confiding, "but you'd know that — I imagine you have the skill of actively listening."

He showed his small, even teeth in a full smile. "You don't have to flatter me, Inspector. I'll tell you everything you want to know. And more, if you like."

"I'll take you up on that, Mr. Carson. Now, could

you start with the last time you met with Ms. Orlando."

Nevile Carson answered efficiently, his gaze never leaving Carol's face. He explained that he had last seen Tala Orlando some weeks before when he had gone to the Orlandel offices to discuss with her and Hayden Delray the pending legal action he was about to launch. Carson's proposal, he told Carol, was that he would agree to drop the suit if Orlandel, in turn, offered him a percentage of the returns for *Take the Risk*. The meeting had ended in a stalemate, with neither side willing to concede anything.

"But the last time I actually spoke to Tala was the morning she died. But you already knew that, didn't you, Inspector?"

"Your mobile number was on the telephone records," Carol said. She was intrigued by his stillness. He made no gestures or body movements and his eyes remained focused on her face. "Where were you when she called you?"

"In my car, on the way to the airport. I was flying to Perth on business and Tala just caught me before I left."

"I'd like the flight details."

A pulse of irritation crossed his face. "The plane was delayed with engine trouble. I didn't actually leave until the afternoon. I'll get you the flight number before you leave. I believe I still have the ticket."

Carol didn't pursue the issue, but made a mental note to check the airline records. She said, "What was Tala's manner like? Did she seem depressed? Upset?"

"I can tell you Tala was certainly not suicidal," he said positively. "She was uncommonly pleasant, actually. Before this whole matter blew up we'd always got on reasonably well, considering the fact that I'd had not only the temerity to divorce her sister, but also to send Robynne into one of her carefully managed declines."

"Managed?" said Carol, curious at the disdain in his voice when he mentioned his ex-wife.

"Indeed, Inspector. Robynne can turn on emotions like a tap, depending on what will get her what she wants, but she doesn't really *feel* anything. I think you'd call it a psychopathic personality, Inspector, but you'd know more about that than I do." He paused, then said with a trace of mockery, "I do hope she hasn't fooled *you*."

Carol let this comment pass, saying, "So was your ex-wife a subject of conversation during this call?"

"No. It was all business — Tala was always all business. It was about *Take the Risk*. She told me she was willing to settle. That she would agree to my terms."

"Settle the action you had against her?" Carol was politely incredulous. "As far as I know, she didn't tell anyone else that, including her husband or her legal advisors."

"Nevertheless, Inspector, it's true," he said flatly. "We needed to sort out the fine details, but I would have accepted Tala's offer. Unfortunately, now that she's dead, I'm going to be forced to go ahead with the legal action. Hayden is far too greedy to be accommodating."

"Did she say she'd discussed this with her

husband? I understand they were equal partners in Orlandel."

A shadow of amusement flickered. "Equal partners?" His pale eyes blinked rapidly. "Legally, perhaps. In reality, no way. Hayden has always liked playing roles that get him attention, and he particularly enjoys the part of media mogul. Unfortunately his abilities don't match his ego."

"Tala thought enough of Hayden Delray to change the name of her company to include his," Carol said smoothly.

"It was a mistake. She regretted it later."

"Do you know that for a fact?"

Carson pursed his lips. "Tala didn't reveal her personal thoughts to me. It's merely my impression." He blinked again. "And for what it's worth, I don't believe Tala's death was an accident. I think she was deliberately killed."

"Murdered? By whom?"

He gave her a slow, sly smile. "Not *me*, Inspector. Surely you can see I had every reason to want Tala alive, and none at all to want her dead." He paused, then added, "Frankly, I'd have a closer look at Robynne, if I were you."

"To be truthful, Carol, Isabel Snipes-More, house cleaner extraordinaire, alarmed me," laughed Bourke as he spooned instant coffee into two mugs. Crammed into the alcove that served the squad as an office kitchen, he seemed larger and more formidable than usual. "She not only took over the interview this morning, she practically convinced me you were a devil-woman."

Carol smiled at him affectionately, thinking that they had worked harmoniously together for so long that now she often took him for granted. But every now and then she was reminded of his humor, his fairness, his quiet control and utter reliability. "We're even, Mark. Nevile Carson alarmed *me.*"

He handed her a mug. "How so?"

"On the surface, very quiet, very mild. The sort that watches and listens. But he's contents under pressure, and I'd say he's a controller from way back. He certainly tried to steer the interview the way he wanted it to go. He depicted his ex-wife as someone with psychopathic tendencies and then mentioned he was sure her sister was murdered."

"Now, there's the problem," said Bourke. "*My* interview went quite the opposite way. Isabel Snipes-More insists that it was all a dreadful accident and that you — apparently because you'll do anything for publicity — are putting the family through hell by even hinting at foul play. She says she tried to tell you so when you saw her, but you wouldn't listen." He grinned at Carol over the rim of his mug. "And as you know, Ms. Snipes-More is a large, square woman with arms like a heavyweight wrestler, so I didn't like to argue with her."

"What about Robynne Orlando?"

"Isabel speaks very highly of her, possibly because, as she explained to me in exhaustive detail, the minimalist furnishings in the house make her job very easy." He made a face as he took a final mouthful of coffee. "It's hard to believe, but this tastes worse than usual." He put his mug in the sink and turned back to Carol. "As for prescription drugs, it seems that Robynne consumes an amazing variety of vitamins, minerals, herbs — you name it. As Isabel describes it, the medicine cabinet is so full of different bottles, boxes and canisters that it looks like a health food store. If there are any tranquilizers, they're lost in the crowd."

"What about the cleaner's original statement? Has she changed her story at all?"

"After Isabel had taken yet another opportunity to lecture me sternly on police incompetence, specifically *yours* in not recognizing that her employer's death was simply a shocking accident, her account corresponded pretty well, with a couple of interesting additions. She started off by running through her schedule, with appropriate comments about the rigors of her job. She cleans the house for Tala Orlando twice a week, and is on call to help tidy up after parties or when there are houseguests. She did her usual clean on Wednesday, then was asked to come in the next day to load the dishwasher and generally clear up after the dinner party the night before. She started at nine o'clock and worked through until one in the afternoon. The only person she saw was her employer. The telephone didn't ring and nobody came to the door. When she first arrived Tala gave her cleaning instructions and said she would be there for an hour or so and was then going out, so would Isabel make sure she locked up when she left. When she didn't see her again she assumed Tala had gone down to the garage, using the inner door, and driven off."

"Surely it wasn't usual for Tala to be there at nine in the morning. I have the impression she spent most of her time at Orlandel."

"You're right, Carol. Isabel was surprised to find her employer at home, since it was customary for her to leave very early for the office."

Carol mentally checked the cleaner's original statement. "Did she mention the alarm system to you?"

"Yes. She repeated the same story — Tala told her not to arm the house alarm when she left."

"If that's true, it's puzzling."

Bourke scratched his sunburnt nose. "Isabel was edgy about the subject. I wonder if she forgot to turn it on, or didn't bother, and now she's covering up."

"Or someone else told her not to set the alarm."

"Is she absolutely sure Hayden Delray wasn't in the house?"

"Isabel Snipes-More —" Bourke rolled the name off his tongue with relish "— is positive that he'd left before she arrived at nine o'clock. But of course she was clearing up in the dining room and kitchen, so anyone could have been in the rest of the house, as long as they kept quiet." Bourke quirked an eyebrow. "And she did assure me several times that Mr. Delray was a very, very nice man."

"You think she'd alter her story to please him?"

"She'd shade it a bit, perhaps. For example, in her written statement she merely said that Tala looked tired that morning. Now we have an expanded version that describes Tala as, to quote Isabel, 'mixed-up, confused and not herself.' Add to that the fact that she's now also conveniently remembered Tala coming into the kitchen about ten o'clock and taking a bottle of Moet out of the refrigerator." He spread his hands. "Call me cynical, but that very neatly fits in with the accident scenario that Delray is peddling — his wife's a little drunk on champagne, a little tired and confused, so when she tosses a Valium or two down her throat and wanders out to her car, it's perfectly feasible that she could start the engine and doze off before she gets around to opening the garage door."

"It could have happened just as you described."

Bourke cocked his head. "Do you believe that, Carol?"

She gave him a grim smile. "I'm beginning to have serious doubts."

"You might be even more doubtful if you speak with Rex and Ruby Courtold about their friendship with Tala. In fact, I'm suggesting you see them yourself, because I'm damn sure they're not being up front with everything." He shrugged. "An instinct, Carol. It's not what they said, it's the way they said it. Their answers were too slick and too rehearsed. They did a great double act, taking it in turns to describe Tala's last dinner party as being the non-event of the century. Nothing happened. No one said anything and there was no conflict. As I remember it, you told me Madeline Shipley had a lively discussion with Tala about the possible re-scheduling of *The Shipley Report,* but apparently that didn't impinge on Rex and Ruby at all. Everything was sweetness and light."

Carol could picture their faces without effort. Rex and Ruby Courtold were grand old troopers of sixties and seventies Australian television, having entertained a generation with comedy and song in a variety show that ran twice a week for years. Though long gone from a regular show on television, their faces were as famously familiar as ever. They had maintained business and personal contacts with the industry that had made them household words, and popped up regularly as guests on talk shows or in bit parts in dramas and comedies.

"Of course I'll see them, but have you any idea what they might be hiding?"

"Not a one." He assumed an expression of mock chagrin. "And I tried everything, Carol, including my famous charm. It didn't work, so I think we need your cold green stare. No one can withstand that for long."

Carol had lunch at her desk. Chewing absentmindedly on a chicken sandwich, she took a blank sheet of paper and printed along the top WHY KILL TALA ORLANDO? She doodled an elaborate garland around the words while she considered the question.

She listed the names — Hayden Delray, Joshua Orlando, Robynne Orlando. After a moment's thought she added Nevile Carson's name.

Hayden Delray — why would he want his successful wife dead? There were rumors of trouble in the marriage. Divorce could be a disaster for him because Tala was both the creative and business force driving Orlandel. Had he resented the fact that there seemed to be a general consensus that he was along for the ride and couldn't hope to emulate his wife's achievements? Money and bitter envy — convincing motives.

Carol looked at the second name. Joshua Orlando appeared unmoved by what to most sons would be a tragedy, but Carol had seen enough bereaved relatives to know that many didn't react in sociably acceptable ways. She'd seen people show their grief in anger, in laughter, in petulant complaint. And many masked their feelings with a show of indifference.

Unless he knew about the recent change to the will that delayed his inheritance until he was thirty, he would have expected his mother's death not only to provide a solution to his present financial problems but also to make him an extremely rich young man.

Third on the list, Robynne Orlando, gave the impression that she was shattered by her sister's death, but if Nevile Carson was to be believed, this could well be an act. Tala had gone out of her way to help her sister after Robynne's marriage had ended, buying Robynne a house next to her own and giving her a job. What would motivate Robynne to kill a caring sister? Money? Jealousy?

Nevile Carson was last, and on the face of it the least likely suspect, presuming he had been telling the truth about Tala's private agreement to settle their conflict over the new quiz show. Carol had a gut feeling he was lying about something — perhaps it was that. And if Tala had never agreed to give Carson a percentage of the profits from *Take the Risk*, then both sides were faced with the crippling costs of a civil action in the courts. Perhaps Carson wanted Tala out of the way because he believed that Hayden Delray would be easier to intimidate into a settlement.

She looked thoughtfully at the list of names. Was the key to Tala's death in those names? She buzzed through to Bourke's desk. "Mark? A couple of things. I want a financial status report on Delray, Tala's son and her sister. And add Nevile Carson. It'd be interesting to know if he has the resources to mount a legal challenge. And will you check how well Joshua is doing at university and what he does with his spare time. Judging from his build, a lot of it must be in a gym somewhere."

As she put down the receiver a young constable came in to hand her an envelope. "Marked urgent, Inspector," he said virtuously. "So I got it to you straight away."

It was the report about Madeline's BMW. Liz had scrawled across the top, "You owe me one, Carol." Apparently, the contents of at least one can of oven cleaner containing caustic soda had been sprayed over the seats and dashboard, followed by a drenching with a mixture of water and chlorine bleach. By itself caustic soda was highly corrosive, but this had been accentuated by the extreme heat generated by the chemical reaction between the oven cleaner and the liquid. In addition, there were no identifiable fingerprints lifted from the interior or exterior of the car.

Carol picked up her phone and punched in a number. Madeline's voice was warm with delight. "Carol! Tell me I am going to see you tonight."

"I'll meet you at the station after your show. For one thing, I've got the report on your car, but I also want to ask you about that last dinner party of Tala's."

"We need to talk about some other things, darling."

"Such as?" Carol was deliberately obtuse.

Madeline gave her tawny laugh. "Don't play dumb. It doesn't suit you. I've got to go. I'll see you at seven-thirty."

As she put down the phone Carol was aware of the tension in her shoulders. She twisted the opal ring she had chosen for herself many years before. Madeline wanted too much from her — and of her. Turning the opal in the light to find the flash of fire hidden in its captivating blue depths, she thought of the diamond and emerald engagement ring and wide gold wedding band that she had taken off with such relief when she had realized her marriage was over. Rings given and received were supposed to be symbols of mutual commitment.

What do they represent to me? Obligation? Possession? She had never worn a ring for Sybil, nor given one to her.

Carol picked up the phone and called her next door neighbor. "Jenny? It's Carol. Would you mind feeding the cats for me? I'm going to be very late tonight."

She spent the next two hours going through the paperwork that threatened to swamp her desk. When she had reduced her in-tray to manageable proportions, she went back to the fat blue file that represented the work on Tala Orlando's death. On the inside cover Bourke had taped a time line. At eight-thirty Hayden Delray had left the house for a business appointment; at nine the cleaner had arrived. Tala had made three telephone calls, one to Nevile Carson at nine twenty-five, one ten minutes later to her son's answering machine, and at ten-thirty one to her assistant, Deena Bush. The cleaner had locked the house and left at one o'clock. At six

Hayden Delray had come home to open the double garage and find the dead body of his wife.

Time of death, based on body temperature and only slight signs of rigor mortis in the body's jaw, was estimated between eleven in the morning and two in the afternoon.

Carol glanced through the post mortem report. Apart from the presence of alcohol, diazepam and a lethal concentration of carbon monoxide, the blood analysis showed a healthy woman with low cholesterol. Carol thought of the care with diet and exercise that had made Tala Orlando so fashionably thin. Carol grimaced. Somehow it seemed ironic to take so much effort and then have it all thrown away.

Where had the tranquilizer come from? And why did Tala, who rarely drank much, have alcohol so early in the day? Did she open a bottle of champagne to celebrate the end of the legal battle between Orlandel and Nevile Carson?

Nevile Carson. Carol reached down and took out the Qantas airline ticket he had given her. He had said his morning flight to Perth had been delayed by engine trouble and he'd waited in the executive lounge at the airport for several hours. The delay gave him plenty of time to drive to Northbridge and see Tala. And of course Carol only had his word that he'd been on his way to the airport when Tala had called him on his mobile phone.

She picked up the receiver, knowing she was in for a succession of irritations as she tried to find the appropriate people at the airport to give her the information she wanted. She was waiting with rising impatience for a clerk to get back on the line when Bourke burst into her office.

"Something's happened to Madeline Shipley. It looks like there's been an attempt on her life. She's been rushed to hospital."

CHAPTER SIX

Kimberley Blackland, her pretty face haloed by thick curly brown hair, was bent solicitously over Madeline's hospital bed. She started when Carol opened the door. "Oh, Inspector Ashton . . . I thought it was the florist. I've ordered absolutely masses of flowers."

Carol had spoken to the doctor and knew that Madeline was out of danger, so even though she was jolted by Madeline's pallor and the drip in her arm, she was amused at Madeline's obvious irritation with the reporter's ministrations. "For God's sake, Kimberley, I won't be here long enough for flowers."

"You're not to worry about the show," Kimberley said soothingly. She patted Madeline's shoulder. "Everything's under control." She adjusted a pillow. "Just tell me if there's anything you want and I'll get it. Do you want me to drop by your house and collect clothes? Makeup?"

"No, Edna's doing that. She'll be here any minute." Madeline made an obvious effort to seem grateful. "But thank you, anyway."

Carol said, "I haven't brought a thing with me. Shall I arrange a selection of fruit?"

Madeline grinned weakly at her ingenuous tone. "Are you a sadist? I'm never going to eat again!"

Kimberley clucked sympathetically. "You'll feel stronger soon." She gave Madeline's shoulder a further comforting pat, then said to Carol, "I've been telling Madeline not to worry about the program tonight or, for that matter, for the rest of the week. Gordon Vaughan's agreed I can step in, so that Madeline can have a good rest."

"I don't need a rest. I'm okay." Madeline tried to sound indignant, but her usually vibrant voice was tenuous. She put out a hand to Carol. "I'm so pleased you're here."

Kimberley was checking her watch. "Madeline, I'll have to run. I mean, there's so much to do before we go to air." She flashed an electric smile at Carol as she gathered her things. "So nice to see you again, Inspector."

When she had gone, Madeline put a hand over her face. "Please tell me she's gone and isn't coming back."

Mock solemn, Carol said, "Kimberley could return any moment with absolutely *masses* of flowers."

Madeline looked through her fingers. "Protect me from her. Please."

Her request sobered Carol. "You may need protection. It seems there's a chance someone tried to poison you. Mark's gone to the channel to organize an analysis of what you ate for lunch. Do you feel strong enough to tell me about it?"

Madeline squeezed her fingers. "I'll tell you anything, darling. Anytime." She frowned. "Aren't you going to take notes?"

"I can see you're feeling better," Carol laughed as she opened her bag to take out a notebook and gold fountain pen.

"Couldn't it just be food poisoning?" Madeline asked hopefully.

"It's possible, but not likely. You told the doctor that you'd skipped breakfast and a late lunch was the first thing you'd eaten today. You began to vomit almost immediately. If you had gastroenteritis from bad food, an hour later is the earliest you'd be affected, and several hours is more likely. And no one else who ate at the canteen is sick."

"If it's deliberate — not an accident — it's him. Marquis." She tried to sit up. "This isn't funny anymore."

"It never was." Carol pushed her gently back into the pillows. "Just relax and tell me what you had for lunch."

"I ordered it from the canteen. I always do when I'm working. Jim went and got the tray for me and put it in my office."

Carol could picture the elegance of Madeline's blue and beige office with its plush carpet and fine furniture. "Were you there when Jim brought in the tray?"

"No, I was down in the studio. It was a chopped salad, so there was no problem about keeping it hot. He just left it on my desk for me. I went up about half an hour later, sat down and ate it."

"What exactly did you order?"

Madeline gave her a faint smile. "They call it the Deluxe Salad Plus. It's quite elaborate, with every kind of salad green and garnish you can imagine and an oil and vinegar dressing."

"It looked the same as usual? There was nothing strange?"

"I didn't pay much attention. I was hungry and I was busy. I was reading something while I was eating. Just thinking about it..." She closed her eyes.

Carol looked down at the notes she had taken when she had interviewed the admitting doctor. *Burning pains in throat and stomach. Numbness in mouth. Dizziness. Extreme thirst. Nausea and violent vomiting.* A pulse of hot anger challenged her composure. She took a deep breath, then said softly, "Try to sleep. I won't ask you any more questions now."

Madeline opened her eyes. "You're not going to leave me, are you?"

"Yes. You need to rest."

Madeline rolled her eyes. "You blew it, Carol," she said with a hint of her customary vigor. "You were supposed to say never, I'll never leave you."

Madeline, you always push too hard, Carol thought as she bent to kiss her cheek. But she found herself smiling as she left the room.

You've no idea how much fun this has been, my Madeline. I hadn't realized how many plants were poisonous until I began my research. Just ordinary houseplants can kill you. Did you know that? Like the leopard lily I have in my living room. Dieffenbachia maculata. It's also called the dumb cane because its sap paralyzes vocal cords so you can't talk. I couldn't do that to you because I love your voice too much. I've been watching you, listening to you. I know everything you do. Everything. I need you to remember you are always speaking for me to hear, moving for me to watch.

I chose my plants very carefully. I found some inside, and some outside. So many different leaves to chop up. I wanted them to look appealing. I think that's important don't you? Food should always look good to eat.

Now you know my power, Madeline. I can take away everything from you. Your speech, your sight, your hearing. Then I'd be your whole world. You'd be dumb, and blind, and deaf. I'd speak, I'd see, I'd hear for you. You cannot guess how tenderly I'd hold you then.

Your Marquis

Rage and apprehension had given Carol a sleepless night. Fragmentary pictures ran in a loop through her mind — Madeline's white face; the huge bunch of orchids delivered to the hospital in the late afternoon with a card that read, *Aren't you sorry, now?;* the letter that had been found at the station in the basket reserved for *The Shipley Report* mail.

Now, sitting in her office, she felt more in control. She took a long swallow of black coffee and put her mug down carefully. "What've you got?" she said to Bourke.

"The flowers from Marquis delivered to the hospital aren't going to get us anywhere. The order was called through and charged to Channel Thirteen, and since Kimberley Blackland had already given them a large order to be delivered to Madeline, this was just assumed to be an additional floral arrangement. The shop was busy and the woman who took the order for the orchids doesn't remember anything at all about the call. In short, it's a dead end. All we can say is that the person knew that Channel Thirteen had an account with that particular florist."

Carol shut her eyes. She felt distanced by fatigue. "What about the salad Madeline ate for lunch?"

"The analysis confirms the information in the letter from our friend," said Bourke. "Two common houseplants, elephant's ear and a sample of monstera deliciosa. Then a nice selection from the garden — oleander, leaves from a member of the daisy family and a poinsettia. Every one of them poisonous."

"Could she have died?" To herself, she sounded

remote, uninterested. Her anger had cooled to a glacial, silent fury.

"The chemist says it was an outside chance, given the amount she ate and the fact she was healthy to begin with. Even so, she was very ill." He grinned at Carol. "It would take more than a toxic salad like this to off our Madeline."

"But he could have chosen things that would have killed her, couldn't he?"

"Sure." Bourke flipped over a page in his notebook. "It's astonishing how many deadly plants there are, including some very pretty flowers. And then there are berries. If he'd decided to grind up the seeds of ornamentals like the castor oil plant or lily-of-the-valley, she would have fallen off her perch for good."

"And the letter was left in the mail room in *The Shipley Report* basket. Definitely hand-delivered?"

"Absolutely. Our guy seems to have free access to the station. He could work there, or visit the studios regularly, for some reason."

"Are we so sure it's a man? It's not written in stone that it has to be."

"A woman?" He pursed his lips. "Well, poisoning *is* a traditional female weapon, but I get the feeling it is a male, and he's on a real power trip. Notice how he talks about all the things he *could* do. He wants to control her by terrifying her."

Carol played with her gold pen. "I don't know . . ."

"Do you have a particular woman in mind?"

"It might be far-fetched, but Kimberley Blackland would do anything to take over *The Shipley Report.*

Madeline was hardly in the ambulance before Kimberley had lined herself up as replacement host. When I got to the hospital she was there assuring Madeline that she should take off as much time as possible."

"Poisoning your boss so you can get more air time — it's a stretch, but I can see it. But Carol, whoever's writing these letters wants a lot more than that."

"There is someone I'd like you to run a check on. Jim Borlie. He just recently started as Madeline's assistant. She says they went to school together, but she hasn't seen him for years. Then he turns up and she gives him a job."

"Could be promising. Mind you, we're not lacking possible suspects. I picked up a staff list yesterday from personnel, as well as the visitors' log at the reception desk. I've asked Anne to run all the names through the computer on the off-chance we score something interesting."

"Security at Channel Thirteen appears okay at this point," said Mark Bourke as he pulled up at one of two boom gates at the entrance to the television station, "but that's all it is — appearance. The place is like a sieve. Anyone who really wanted to could get in."

A uniformed guard stepped out of his booth and came to the driver's window with a clipboard. "Who will you be seeing, sir, and do you have an appointment?"

Mark showed his identification. "Detective Inspector Ashton and I have an appointment with Gordon Vaughan."

The guard handed him the clipboard. "If you'd just fill in your details, sir."

Bourke complied and handed the form back to the guard, who opened the boom gate and let them through.

"See what I mean, Carol? The guard didn't call ahead to verify we actually had an appointment and he only glanced at my identification and didn't ask to see yours." He glanced at Carol sitting beside him in a tailored charcoal suit and dark green silk shirt that matched the color of her eyes. "Of course, we both *do* look impressive, dressed up in our best for the funeral this afternoon."

Bourke turned into the visitors' car park and pulled up near the angular mustard-yellow building that had a huge scarlet CHANNEL THIRTEEN across its windowless exterior. *All Visitors,* announced a large sign above double glass doors.

Carol got out of the car and looked around. Attempts at landscaping with clumps of native bushes had failed to beautify the essential ugliness of the angular building but did provide cover for concealment. "Mark, what are the perimeter fences like?"

"Inadequate. Anyone could get over them."

"Is there security on other entrances?"

Bourke shook his head. "It's pretty lax. I had a good look around when I was here yesterday. Once you're on the grounds you can pretty much do what you like." He pointed to a wide drive that disappeared down one side of the building. "Come and have a look."

No one challenged them as they walked around to a large loading dock. It was wide open and deserted. Inside Carol could see racks and scaffolding. "Scenery, flats, that sort of stuff," said Bourke, following her glance. "Anyone could walk in, no questions asked."

"Excuse me. What are you doing here?" said a hard voice.

Bourke looked behind him, then turned and grinned at Carol. "Well, well. I spoke too soon. There is some semblance of security."

The man was wearing an ordinary gray suit, but a large yellow and scarlet badge on his lapel proclaimed *Channel Thirteen Security*. He had a compact body, a tight face and a pugnacious manner. "You've no authority to be here. I'll have to ask you to come with me." He looked closely at Carol and his manner changed. "It's Inspector Ashton, isn't it? I'm sorry, I didn't recognize you."

"We're just looking at your security arrangements," said Carol.

The man gave a sharp bark of laughter. "Some arrangements! That's what I'm here to do. Tighten them up." He gestured scornfully at the open dock. "Look at this. It's a disaster."

"I suppose this is because of what happened to Madeline Shipley?" said Bourke.

"Too right it is! Vaughan put me on it this morning, first thing. Is that who you're here to see? Yes? I'll take you there." He strode rapidly over to the metal steps that ran up one side of the dock, obviously expecting them to follow him immediately.

Over his shoulder he said, "Name's Parsons. Eddie Parsons. Head of security for the Shearing Corporation. Been brought in to clear this mess up."

This part of the building was a maze of passageways, studios and storage areas, but Parsons led them without hesitation until the spartan conditions changed to an executive affluence that Carol recognized from previous visits.

Parsons gestured to a small glassed sitting room with a television monitor chattering away to empty leather chairs. "If you just wait here I'll check that Mr. Vaughan's in his office."

"I'd like a full check on Mr. Parsons," said Carol. "I'd hate it if we had a wolf guarding a lamb."

"Madeline Shipley a lamb?" laughed Bourke. "She'd eat him for breakfast."

CHAPTER SEVEN

Gordon Vaughan's office was almost military in its uncluttered, practical lines. His mahogany desk was clear of any documents and there were no curtains at the window or any concessions to decoration. His manner as he came forward to greet them was brisk, authoritative. "I can give you twenty-five minutes. No more." He waved Carol and Bourke toward heavy leather chairs set around a plain functional coffee table and gestured for Eddie Parsons to leave.

As he settled himself opposite them, Carol studied him. He was wearing a navy suit and dark red tie.

He looked imposing, and he knew it. His hooked nose and strong jawline gave him a combative air and his heavy shoulders and height made him formidable.

Carol had read a brief summary of Gordon Vaughan's career and knew that he was accustomed to success. In his youth a record-holding Olympic butterfly swimmer for Australia, he had retired from competitive sport to take a lowly position at a television station in the small market of Perth, Western Australia. Using that experience as a springboard, he had steadily worked his way up through different networks, switching to larger markets whenever an opportunity presented itself. On the way he had married the daughter of a media magnate and this family connection had not hindered his rise to higher management positions. His wife had died in a car accident three years previously. They had had no children.

His last promotion had put him in charge of the most important Australian television station in the Shearing Corporation Network. He seemed to be strategically positioning himself to move into network management, possibly in Shearing's growing overseas interests.

Gordon Vaughan waited until Parsons had closed the door behind him. "Since it's clear whoever attacked Madeline is extremely dangerous, I've tightened security throughout the station and arranged for a state-of-the-art alarm system to be installed in her house as soon as possible."

"Ms. Shipley will still be vulnerable when she's driving her car," said Bourke.

Vaughan waved this away. "Not a problem. Eddie

Parsons is on to it. Until this psycho is caught, she'll be chauffeured by a trained driver." He glanced at his watch. "Because of the funeral this afternoon, I have very little time now, so perhaps you could check these matters with Parsons after we finish. Now, Inspector, what did you want to ask me about Tala?"

"On Sunday I watched the program Channel Thirteen ran on her life. It was very laudatory, but it incorporated part of an earlier program that had been very critical of Ms. Orlando, to the point where I believe she threatened to sue your company for defamation and —"

"Tala never carried through with any legal action against us," he interrupted. "I don't know if you realize this, Inspector, but the threats she made were just standard window dressing for the public. I hadn't joined Channel Thirteen at that point, but I know my predecessor only authorized the program for broadcast after Tala had had an opportunity to review it. Predictably, she hated it and demanded it not be shown, but the network lawyers gave the opinion it wasn't actionable once a couple of things were modified, so it went to air." He gave a satisfied smile. "Got huge ratings. Anything about Tala Orlando is hot."

"So her death's been good for ratings?" said Bourke.

Vaughan shot him an impatient look. "I'm very close to Tala and Hayden. Tala was originally a friend of my late wife's — that's how long I've known her. But I'm in the business of giving viewers what they want, and they have an insatiable appetite for anything about Tala Orlando. That means on a commercial level I make decisions that have nothing to do with my personal feelings." Vaughan switched his attention back to Carol. "What else?" he demanded.

"The dinner party," said Carol. Vaughan drummed his fingers on his knee as she consulted her notebook. He was attempting to run the interview, and Carol wanted to regain control by making him wait. At last she said, "Apart from yourself, the guest list included Robynne Orlando, Madeline Shipley, Rex and Ruby Courtold. Of course Ms. Orlando and Mr. Delray were also there, but was anyone else?"

"Tala's assistant — what's her name? Deena, I think. She was there for a while, but she didn't eat with us."

Carol asked him a series of questions about the evening to ascertain the topics of conversation and the interrelationships between the diners. Vaughan answered with growing irritation, finally snapping, "I fail to see why any of this is important, Inspector."

Imperturbable, Carol said, "We're interested in Ms. Orlando's state of mind."

Bourke broke in, "You're a close friend. What was your take on their marriage?"

"Like most marriages, there were good times and bad. I was fond of Tala, but she could be difficult. She never would let Hayden forget that she controlled the company and made all the decisions. Naturally he resented that, so of course there was tension between them at times." He waited for a moment, then said, "To be frank, Inspector, just before she died Tala was talking to me about a legal separation."

"Had she actually taken any steps — seen a lawyer, for instance."

"No. She was just talking about it. Maybe Tala was serious. Maybe not. I don't know."

Carol unscrewed the cap of her gold pen. "Channel Thirteen has been negotiating with Orlandel Productions about *Take the Risk,* the new quiz show that's been sold overseas and looks like it's going to be a huge success. I gather Ms. Orlando's company would produce the Australian version and you would telecast it. Isn't that the case?"

"Indeed. The contract was all but signed when Tala died." He settled back comfortably in his seat. "We intend to show the program throughout Australia on our network. No doubt matters will be finalized shortly."

"However, there's a problem, isn't there?" Carol's tone was polite inquiry.

He smiled affably. "In this business there are always problems."

"But this particular problem is a major headache for you."

He sat forward, frowning. "I don't know where you get your information, Inspector, but I can assure you that we will be signing a contract with Orlandel in the very near future."

"Madeline Shipley's program runs on your channel Monday to Friday at seven o'clock each night." Carol consulted her notes. "Correct me if I'm wrong, but I gather Tala Orlando was demanding that the *Take the Risk* contract between your companies include a clause that would guarantee that her new quiz show would be strip-programmed at that same time because her research indicated it would get the best ratings in that position. In other words, she was asking you to move *The Shipley Report* from its established time slot. And I understand Madeline Shipley is unhappy about the idea."

He spread his hands. "Stars are always unhappy about something. It goes with talent, I suppose."

Remembering Madeline's anger as she had explained to Carol what she thought the move to a different time slot would do to her show's ratings, Carol thought that *ferociously angry* would be a more accurate description of Madeline's reaction.

Carol said thoughtfully, "In fact, Mr. Vaughan, Madeline Shipley claims she has an agreement with your station that the seven o'clock slot is guaranteed to *The Shipley Report*."

Vaughan lifted his heavy shoulders. "I must say none of this has the importance you seem to give it. The whole issue of the time slot for *Take the Risk* was merely an item for negotiation, among many others. And I have to point out that I can't imagine any television company agreeing to have its programming controlled by an independent production company, even one as successful as Tala Orlando's."

"But surely," said Carol with polite astonishment, "that is exactly what you were going to have to do if you wanted to obtain this potentially high-rating quiz show. Our information is that Tala Orlando was also negotiating with a rival network — one that doesn't have your scheduling problems at seven o'clock."

"Seems like a dilemma to me," said Bourke cheerfully. "Whatever you did, you were in trouble." He looked inquiringly at Vaughan. "Is Hayden Delray as hard-nosed as his wife was?"

There was a click as someone turned the handle of the office door. "Gordon, darling, I —" Kimberley Blackland stopped abruptly. "Oh, I didn't realize..."

Vaughan's face was expressionless. "I'm sure whatever it is can wait, Kimberley. Now, if you don't mind..." He immediately turned back to Carol and Bourke, ignoring Kimberley's red-faced retreat. "About Hayden, I can't possibly tell you about his negotiating style at this point in time. He's lost his wife in tragic circumstances. He has to get through the ordeal of her funeral this afternoon. The last thing he would be concerned about at the moment is the fine details of a contract."

"From your point of view it might seem a perfect time to negotiate with him," said Bourke.

Vaughan checked his watch again and pushed back his chair. "I'm sorry, I have an important appointment." Pointedly ignoring Bourke, he said to Carol, "If you have other questions, perhaps we can handle them on the phone."

After he had ushered them out of his office and they were walking down the blue-carpeted corridor, Bourke said to Carol, "So Kimberley Blackland's on intimate terms with the big boss. Sounds like the casting-couch route to success to me."

"It might encourage her to think she'd be the replacement if Madeline couldn't continue *The Shipley Report*." She stopped as they came to the rabbit warren of rooms that made up the general office area. "If I know you, Mark, when you were here yesterday you ingratiated yourself with everyone from the receptionist up."

Bourke grinned at her ironic tone. "How could you doubt it? We both know you go to the real workers in an organization when you want the good oil. And they've got a pretty efficient office telegraph here. Most people knew about the Marquis letter being found in the mail room."

Carol looked at him with amused affection. "Okay, Mark, let's see how good you really are. Find out if there's any gossip about Kimberley Blackland and Gordon Vaughan. And try Tala Orlando's name, too. While you're doing that, I'm going to find Jim Borlie." As Bourke turned away, Carol added, "And in case I forget... Don't give it first priority, but I would like to know exactly how Gordon Vaughan's first wife died."

When Carol opened the door to Madeline's office, Jim Borlie looked up from behind Madeline's sleek desk. "Inspector!" He slammed a drawer and got quickly to his feet. "I didn't expect you." He seemed discomforted, his soft-featured face flushed. "I was just organizing things. Madeline's saying she wants to get back to work on Monday, but I can't think she's serious. It's too soon, isn't it?"

"I spoke to Madeline this morning. Her doctor says she can leave hospital tomorrow, which gives her the weekend to recover before Monday's show." Carol gave him a friendly smile. "When she's absolutely determined to do something, I think you know nothing can stop her."

Borlie tapped his fingers against his lips, and Carol was struck again by the smallness of his hands. "I do believe Kimberley was counting on doing the show next week too." His voice had a hint of malicious amusement. "I'll have to tell her Madeline will definitely be back on Monday."

As he began to gather up a bundle of folders, Carol said, "Where exactly did you put the lunch tray yesterday?"

"Why, right here, on Madeline's desk. I often pick up lunch for her. It's always something cold, so I don't worry if she isn't here. The meal was covered, her coffee was in an insulated jug — there was no reason not to leave it." He looked anxious. "Everything was just as usual."

"It's obvious the salad was tampered with after it left the canteen." Carol's tone wasn't accusatory, but Borlie bit his lip and stared at the floor.

"I blame myself," he said bitterly. "I mean, I knew she was getting those letters. If only I'd stayed in the office, or maybe called Madeline and told her I'd collected her lunch . . ." He looked at Carol. "It's this Marquis guy, isn't it? *He* did it."

"You haven't heard about the letter hand-delivered to the mail room? I'm surprised, I thought it was common knowledge."

Borlie's mouth tightened. "I don't listen to office gossip, Inspector. Now, what else would you like to know?"

Carol took him through the details of when and where he'd collected the tray and how long it had been unattended on the desk. "So there was a period of at least half an hour where there was an opportunity to poison the salad?"

"Well, the door is never locked, so anyone could come in. Of course, every visitor has to wear an identification tag." Borlie looked at her hopefully. "Maybe someone saw a stranger in the corridor . . . ?"

"Can you think of any person here at the station who might want to harm her?"

Borlie looked horrified. "*Here?* That's absolutely impossible. Surely you don't seriously think that it's someone Madeline works with!"

"We have to consider all possibilities," said Carol smoothly. "This is an industry with a lot of big egos, ambitious people and —"

The door slammed open. "Here you are!" Eddie Parsons sounded irritated. He gestured impatiently. "I must see you before you leave."

"Use this office, if you like," said Jim Borlie. "I have to go down to production." Clutching folders to his chest, he hurried out the door.

Parsons made himself comfortable on one of the plump, blue leather chairs, leaning forward to rest his elbows on his spread knees. "Inspector," he said confidently, "since you're investigating Tala Orlando's death, I know you've been considering whether she was murdered or not. But have you made any connection between her death and what happened to Madeline Shipley yesterday?"

Carol raised her eyebrows. "What possible connection could there be?"

"Well, obviously none, if Orlando's death was an accident, or suicide, but if it was something more sinister, then the attack on Shipley could be linked."

"Do *you* think it was murder?" asked Carol.

"It's not as if I'm a friend of the family," said Parsons with a satisfied smile. "But I did have something to do with them. Did you know that Mr. Vaughan arranged for me to do a full safety check on the Orlando house and oversee the updating of the whole security system?" He seemed pleased when she shook her head. "So you might say I had an insider's eye on the situation."

"What situation was that?"

"Frosty. Very frosty. Delray and his wife didn't get on at all. Oh, they were polite in front of me, but I could tell there was tension there." He put a finger against the side of his nose. "A convenient death. Didn't smell right."

"Do you have any hard information?"

"Well, no, just a feeling."

"And this link between Madeline Shipley and Tala Orlando?"

"Look, Inspector, you have to admit it's a bit of a stretch to think there are two killers out there acting independently. First Orlando's murdered, then there's an attempt on Shipley's life. There *has* to be a connection."

"If we accept what you're saying is right, then the situation would be that Marquis, the man who's stalking Madeline Shipley, also murdered Tala Orlando. At the moment I can't see anything that links them."

Parsons leaned back and folded his arms. "I can't pretend to do your job for you, Inspector, but I wouldn't ignore the possibility."

There was a knock at the door, and Jim Borlie bustled in. "Sorry to interrupt, but I forgot something." He snatched a folder from the desk.

Eddie Parsons watched him go with undisguised scorn. "There was no proper background check on Borlie," he snorted. "Personnel just took Shipley's word that she knew him years ago."

"I assume *you* have done a check."

"Too right, I have. As soon as I got here yesterday I ran everyone who had anything to do with Shipley. Borlie's an inadequate little bastard." He held up his hand and began to tick off points on his thick square fingers. "One, Borlie's never married. Doubt if he's ever had a girlfriend. Two, he still lives with his mother. Three, although he knows television — he should, he's had enough jobs in the industry — he's never got anywhere. Assistant to someone is the best he'll ever be." He smiled smugly. "Not bad for the time I had to do it, eh? Want any more?"

"Anything you can tell me." Carol made sure she sounded appreciative. It was clear Parsons enjoyed being the source of information, and she wanted to encourage him to talk.

"Right! I'm sure you'll be interested to know his hobby is porno stuff — tapes, magazines, the whole works. And he's had two episodes of mental illness serious enough to put him in hospital."

"You have hard information?"

He puffed up a little. "Of course. I can give you all the details, doctors' names, everything..."

Tala Orlando's funeral was held at the fashionable church she had attended sporadically. The crowds spilled over into the street, competing with television crews and a gaggle of reporters for space. There was a roped corridor for those going to the service, but they ran the gauntlet of curious eyes and shouted questions.

Inside, the church was packed with Tala Orlando's friends, colleagues, and a stellar selection of media management and talent. There was a smattering of politicians, including the Federal Minister for Communications, who, aware an election wasn't far off, had managed to get a pithy sound bite in before entering the building.

Permission had been given for the service to be videotaped, and the crew that would give a feed to all the other stations had set their equipment up at the back of the church, their casual jeans in strong contrast to the clothing of most of the mourners.

Bourke and Carol had arrived early, but not soon enough to avoid the ubiquitous media. "Inspector Ashton! Was it murder?" Ignoring the microphones shoved in front of her, Carol had walked quickly into the church with Bourke. The casket was richly shining dark wood bearing a simple spray of red roses. Banks of flowers crowded the sanctuary, and a robed choirmaster was putting music folders into the choir stalls. There was a discreet hum of conversation, almost drowned out by suitably solemn organ music.

The pews were only now beginning to fill, so she and Bourke took a seat near the front, directly behind the family group. Hayden sat next to the main aisle and beside him was Robynne, head bent. On her other side Joshua looked around with cool interest, and next to him Carol recognized the elderly, perfectly turned out couple as Rex and Ruby Courtold.

Bourke had been inspecting the congregation. "Tala seems to have known everyone in town."

Carol kept her voice low. "A lot of people owed

her favors, and vice versa. And it's clear she made a lot of enemies. She also moved in on a couple of smaller competitors and swallowed them whole. There'll be people here who are pleased to attend her funeral."

In front of them Robynne Orlando surged to her feet. "What are you doing here?" She swayed against her brother-in-law, who had also risen.

Nevile Carson said mildly, "I thought I should sit with the family. Tala was my sister-in-law."

The man's matter-of-fact tone seemed to incense Hayden. His face flushed, he ground out, "Have some decency and get out." Then, becoming aware that the scene was exciting interest, not only in the other mourners, but also with the camera crew, he dropped his voice to say, "I don't care what you do, but you can't sit with us."

Carson looked past him to his ex-wife. "My condolences, Robynne." He went to the other side of the aisle and squeezed in at the end of a pew.

Robynne sank down. "I can't cope, Hayden. I can't cope." Her nephew looked at her with clinical interest as Hayden murmured something calming.

Kimberley Blackland was making an entrance. She hurried down the aisle wearing a well-cut dark suit and a serious expression. "Robynne. I saw. Nevile has no right. You must be so upset." She swept past Hayden Delray and sank down beside Robynne. A moment to comfort her, then she leaned across Robynne to touch Joshua Orlando's hand and say, "Josh! I tried to get you last night."

"I was out."

"Perhaps later?"

"Maybe. I'll get back to you."

Carol saw Kimberley's mouth tighten at Joshua's offhand tone, but she didn't respond. After a moment she turned to Hayden Delray. "Madeline can't be here. You've heard?"

"She called. She's ill." He wasn't interested.

"Terribly ill," said Kimberley. She added virtuously, "But recovering quickly, thank God."

Carol's attention was taken from the conversation by an agitated Deena Bush, who appeared at the end of her pew. "Inspector, can I sit with you? There's something I have to tell you."

Bourke raised an eyebrow to Carol as he shuffled along to make room. Deena seated herself between them and immediately took out a handful of tissues. The organ music swelled, the muted conversation faded and the choir processed into the church.

Tears had begun to flow from Deena's eyes. She dabbed at her cheeks with the wad of tissues. "I didn't tell you everything," she said softly to Carol. She looked at the family group in front of them and leaned closer. "What I didn't tell you," she whispered, "was that Tala and her sister had a dreadful fight that night, before she died."

CHAPTER EIGHT

Aunt Sarah, her plump form resplendent in iridescent green overalls and a chrome-yellow blouse, frowned over the breakfast dishes at Carol. "You were in very late last night, Carol. Work?"

"Yes, I had a lot to do after the Orlando funeral, and then I visited Madeline in hospital." She didn't add that she'd then been to see Edna, Madeline's housekeeper, to review the security of Madeline's house and to ask her if she'd noticed any strangers hanging around in the last few weeks. And then

Carol, tired though she was, had gone back to her office to work another couple of hours.

"Madeline Shipley." Aunt Sarah's tone was disapproving. She flapped the pages of the morning paper she was reading. "She's made almost as big a splash as Tala Orlando's funeral. Is it true someone tried to poison her at the television station?" She turned the page so Carol could see the headline, POISONED STAR FIGHTS FOR LIFE. "Or is it just a publicity stunt?"

Topping up her mug from her battered coffee percolator, Carol said firmly, "It's not a stunt. She's being stalked."

Carol's aunt looked doubtful. "You sure, dear? Media personalities will do just about anything for publicity."

"I'm sure." Carol knew of several cases where people in the public eye had set up elaborate hoaxes to generate even more attention, but she couldn't believe that Madeline would initiate a campaign of anonymous letters and then poison herself. "For months he's been sending her flowers and letters. Now he's actually attacked her."

"So it says here. The reporter calls it a 'reign of terror.' " Aunt Sarah's expression was skeptical. "I see Madeline's well enough to do an interview from her hospital bed." She peered at the page. "She's being very brave, and . . ." She handed Carol the newspaper folded to present a photograph of Madeline in bed, surrounded by flowers. ". . . very photogenic." She added sardonically, "She certainly couldn't buy the coverage she's been getting. Is her contract with Channel Thirteen up for review?"

"You don't like Madeline, do you, Aunt?"

Aunt Sarah ran her fingers through her cloud of white hair. "I don't think she's good for you." A look of chagrin crossed her face. "Hell's bells!" she said. "Forget I said that. I promised myself I wouldn't interfere."

Carol leaned back and folded her arms. "I suppose you're going to mention Sybil next."

"What would you do if Sybil walked in that door, right now?"

"She's in England."

"That's not an answer."

What would I do? Carol slid off the stool at the breakfast bar. "I thought you said you wouldn't interfere."

Aunt Sarah grinned at her. "Sorry, darling. I'll try not to do it again." She gathered plates and bustled over to the sink. "Aren't you having David this weekend? I can fit in a movie, if he's free."

Carol shook her head. "I canceled. David understands how busy I am. I'll make it up to him as soon as I get the Orlando case out of the way."

Her aunt frowned at her. "He's twelve, Carol. He'll be grown up before you know it, and you've already missed so much of his childhood." Before Carol could respond, Aunt Sarah threw up her hands. "I know! I know! I'm interfering again." She smiled ruefully. "The rally starts at ten. I'll go and interfere with the French intentions to test nuclear devices in the Pacific. *That's* a lot less dangerous."

* * * * *

Robynne Orlando didn't hide her displeasure. Her navy blue dress and perfectly applied makeup suggested that she was ready to go out. "I can't imagine why you want to see me yet *again,* Inspector Ashton." She looked at Carol's casual slacks and deep rose shirt with disfavor, then seated herself in the same leather and metal chair that she had occupied during the last interview. Motioning Carol to the angular couch, she said, "I thought I made it plain on the phone that this really isn't convenient. Hayden will be here any moment."

The morning sunshine glanced through the huge windows in dazzling shafts, making the room's furnishings seem even more sparse. "I'm sorry to disturb you, but further information has made it necessary," Carol said with professional sincerity.

Robynne clasped her hands so tightly her knuckles showed white. "Yesterday — the funeral." She turned her head away. "You must realize that this is a very hard time for me."

Carol considered her narrowly. Was she acting, as Nevile Carson maintained, or was she genuinely grief-stricken? "Your ex-husband was at the funeral."

Robynne's head whipped around. "You saw what he tried to do! He thinks he's still *family.*" She gave the final word a scornful emphasis.

"Mr. Carson told me that your sister was willing to settle the dispute about *Take the Risk* with him by giving him an equitable share of the profits. Did she say anything to you about that?"

"He's lying." Her tone was vicious. "Nevile's always been a liar. I only found out after I married him that he'd always prefer to tell a lie rather than the truth."

"Was that why you divorced?" Carol was all polite inquiry.

Her lips pressed tightly together, Robynne stared at her. At last she said, "I don't see why it's any of your business, but Tala found out Nevile had been cheating her in the business. My sister trusted him completely, but then she discovered that he'd been leaking the best of our program concepts to competitors." She lifted her chin. "You can see why I couldn't stay married to a man like that!"

"You're very loyal to your sister."

Robynne looked at her sharply, but Carol kept her face expressionless. "Tala is — was — everything to me. When Nevile betrayed her, he betrayed me."

Carol said sympathetically, "The divorce was very hard on you . . ."

Robynne's face crumpled. "It was. I couldn't believe it, you see." She blinked rapidly to clear the tears that filled her eyes. "But when I realized Nevile had lied and lied . . . Our marriage was over." She looked down at the floor.

Hoping that a sudden change of direction would shock her into an unguarded response, Carol said abruptly, "You had a serious argument with your sister the night before she died."

Robynne jerked up her head. "Who told you that?"

"Is it true?"

"Deena. It's Deena Bush, isn't it?" Her face had grown hard. "She's going to be fired any day now, so she's causing trouble. I don't know why Tala kept her on. I told her over and over Deena was hopeless."

"Are you saying it isn't true? Our informant says, to quote, 'it was a dreadful fight.' "

The lines of Robynne's face seemed to have grown sharper. "Tala and I didn't have a fight. I've already told you she was edgy and irritable, so if someone overhead us talking, the way Tala said something might have sounded like we were having an argument. We weren't." She snapped off the last two words, then glared at Carol.

There were heavy footsteps in the hall. Robynne immediately got to her feet. "That'll be Hayden." She raised her voice to call, "Hayden, we're in here. Inspector Ashton was just going."

Although Robynne was obviously waiting for her to stand up, Carol remained seated. Hayden Delray stopped in the doorway. His face was flushed and a graze on his chin showed he had cut himself shaving. "Inspector Ashton," he said coldly. His resonant voice rang in the room.

He advanced deliberately until his bulk loomed over her. "I don't mind telling you I'm surprised you would intrude on a grieving family this way."

The helpful manner of the earlier interviews had disappeared. Carol was sure his bellicose stance and tight expression were intended to intimidate. She said mildly, "I'm following up new information."

"It's Deena Bush," hissed Robynne. "She's trying to cause trouble. She's saying Tala and I had a fight the day before she died."

"I see." His high color seemed to intensify as he put his face closer to Carol's. "I'm getting very tired

103

of this, Inspector Ashton. It almost seems as though you're finding any excuse to avoid closing the case. Tala's funeral is over, but there's still no resolution concerning the way she died." He paused to let his words sink in, then added with slow, heavy emphasis, "So I expect that you will come to the conclusion that her death was an accident. Then we can all get on with our lives."

Carol leaned back in the uncomfortable chair, as if she were at ease. "But Mr. Delray," she said coolly, "I'm far from convinced that your wife's death was accidental. In fact, I feel sure at least one other person was involved."

He stepped back, passing his hand through his sandy hair. "You can't be serious!" His fleshy face showed equal parts of anger and consternation.

Carol stood. He was only slightly taller, so they were almost eye to eye. "I'm perfectly serious," she said. "And I know I can count on your cooperation."

"At last!" Madeline got up from the chair beside her hospital bed. Although she was pale, she seemed to have regained some of her usual vivacity. "Let's get out of here, darling."

Carol gestured at the abundance of flowers that crowded the room. "Do you want to take any of these with you?"

Madeline's smile faded. "Not after the orchids from Marquis and the card asking me if I was sorry. Anyway, I expect some people have sent flowers to the house."

"For your own safety I don't want you to take

delivery of *anything* at either Channel Thirteen or at home. No flowers, no packages, nothing. I've already spoken to Edna about it. And don't let any stranger into your house, no matter who they say they are."

"My house?" Madeline stared at her. "You really think he'd try to get to me at home?"

"Why not? You're not protected there. Gordon Vaughan told me he's arranged for an alarm system to be installed, but until that happens, anyone could break in."

Madeline's flash of energy was exhausted. She leaned against Carol, her head only coming to Carol's shoulder. Feeling unexpectedly protective, Carol put an arm around her. "You could stay in a hotel until the security system is in. Frankly, I'd feel happier if you did."

Madeline looked up at her with entreaty in her smile. "*You* could come home and stay with me, Carol. Then I'd be safe."

Carol said quickly, "That's not possible." Surprising herself with her terse rejection of Madeline's proposal, Carol added in a more conciliatory voice, "I couldn't be there most of the time. You need to be protected twenty-four hours a day until we catch him."

"Catch him? Do you have any ideas who it is?"

"I want to go through that with you, but let's get you home first."

Madeline groaned when they reached the foyer of the hospital and saw a media contingent waiting. "I don't believe it!" As they converged on her, she raised her voice to say, "Give me a break."

A reporter holding a Channel Thirteen microphone laughed. "Not a chance, Madeline."

Carol stood back, and with resigned grace Madeline submitted to the attention. "I'm feeling much better ... Yes, I'll be back on air on Monday ... I have no idea exactly how it happened, but I can say it wasn't an accident ..."

Carol was cynically amused at the thought that if Madeline was hoping to avoid exposure of their friendship, having the media discover her leaving hospital on Carol's arm was hardly the way to go.

When Carol finally got her to the refuge of the car, Madeline sank gratefully into the passenger seat with a sigh. "I didn't need that."

Pulling out into the stream of traffic, Carol automatically scanned to see if any other vehicle seemed to be following. "It's a change for you to be on the receiving end, isn't it?"

Her wry tone brought an instant response. "Just what is that supposed to mean?" Madeline said indignantly. "Are you saying that just because I interview people for a living, I should put up with it myself, no matter how I feel?"

Carol had seen Madeline probe and dissect hapless interviewees too often to feel too much sympathy. "Try to imagine how someone feels who has just had a tragedy in the family, or witnessed something grisly."

Madeline glared at her. "*You* ask people questions all the time in situations like that. And I don't suppose you considerately wait until they're feeling better, do you?"

"There's no comparison." Carol checked the rear vision mirror again. Was that white car the same one that had been behind them just after they'd left the hospital?

"Of course there's a comparison." Madeline shot her a triumphant look. "For one thing, we both get paid to ask questions."

Carol braked, abruptly turning left off the main route. The white car didn't follow. "Sorry. Thought someone might be following us."

Madeline twisted around to look out the back window. "You're not talking about reporters, are you?" She turned back and put a hand on Carol's arm. "You're scaring me. Do you really think he'd follow us in broad daylight?"

Carol took a sharp left, then a right. "If he's there, I'd like to know. Many stalkers get a kick out of shadowing their targets unseen because it gives them feelings of being invisible, of having ultimate power. They often take photographs to enjoy later."

"Carol, you *are* scaring me."

Carol gave Madeline's hand a brief squeeze. "Good. That should make you very careful."

Returning to the main road, she continued to scan the traffic without any real hope that she would detect anything suspicious. She knew that it was just as likely that Marquis would stake out Madeline's home, sure that she would return there, if for nothing else to pack a suitcase before she moved out. "You won't reconsider, Madeline? You could pick up some clothes and I could drive you to a hotel."

"Not a chance." Madeline set her jaw. "No one's going to frighten me out of my own house."

Carol glanced at her when they stopped at a red light. Madeline, staring out the window, looked tired and drawn. It was clear that she was more shaken and frightened than she would admit. Carol wanted to put her arms around her and tell her everything was all right. But of course, it wasn't. Carol clenched her teeth. *Just one mistake, you bastard, and I'll have you.*

As the traffic moved, Madeline said with an effort at lightness, "After you left the hospital last night, I saw you on the news, darling, looking stunning as usual."

Although she hadn't watched television last night, Carol was sure Tala Orlando's funeral had been featured on all the network newscasts. "It was quite a social event."

"I see they even got Nevile on camera. That was an achievement."

"Do you know him well?"

"Reasonably well. I first met him when he was married to Tala's sister, though after they divorced he pretty well dropped out of sight. And lately I've seen him several times at Channel Thirteen when he's come to see Gordon. Actually, he approached me with an idea he had for a sitcom where I'd play — would you believe — the host of a news magazine show." She mockingly framed her face with her hands. "See this face? Nevile said I would have an instantaneous recognition factor."

"I didn't know you aspired to act."

"I don't. I told him thanks, but no thanks. He gave me a hard sell but quit when it was obvious I wasn't interested." She chuckled. "Of course, when she heard about the offer, Kimberley told Nevile that she was *very* interested in acting. She wasn't pleased when he turned her down."

"What do you think of him?"

"An enigma. Quiet, but watchful. I like him."

Madeline laughed. "But then, darling, I always like people who let me do most of the talking."

Madeline's live-in housekeeper opened the front door, then stood back to let them in. Edna's gray hair was pulled back in a tight bun, and although not tall, she held herself with a military rigidity. In all the time she had known her, Carol had never seen her smile fully — the most Carol had observed was a slight twitching of Edna's thin lips.

She acknowledged Carol, then said to Madeline, "Are you well enough to be home?" Her tone indicated she doubted that this was the case.

"Of course I am, Edna," said Madeline briskly. "Is it warm enough, do you think, for Carol and me to have lunch outside?"

"Maybe." Edna preceded them down the hallway. She said over her shoulder, "It'll be a while before lunch is ready, so I'll bring you out a tray with coffee and cake."

Madeline grinned at Carol as Edna disappeared into the kitchen. "I've learned not to argue with her. Whether we want coffee and cake or not, that's what we'll get."

It was pleasant to sit outside sipping coffee and looking at the sweep of lawn and the late-flowering bushes in the private back garden. The ornamental grape vine that formed a shady arbor in summer had lost its leaves in autumn, and the sun dappled the ground in warm pools.

"You knew Tala well," Carol said, "so I wonder what you think about the rumor that she was having an affair."

"An affair?" Madeline considered. "Things were

cool between Hayden and Tala, but I always thought that was because his ego was bruised — she was so obviously the driving force behind the company." She smiled at Carol. "If Tala was having an affair, she certainly didn't confide in me. But then, she wouldn't over something like that. Even though we were friends, she was always very conscious that I was in the media."

"She didn't trust you to be quiet?"

This amused Madeline. "Tala didn't trust *anyone.*"

A chime sounded from the direction of the kitchen. "That's the front door," said Madeline. "Edna's getting a bit deaf, so it rings at the back of the house too."

Carol was already on her feet. "When I saw Edna yesterday I told her not to answer the door unless she was absolutely sure she knew who it was. I'll just check she's taken me seriously. Be back in a moment."

When she returned to the garden, Madeline was grave. "I've always felt safe in this house. Nothing could hurt me here. But now..." She looked up as Carol sat down. "Who was it at the door? Not more flowers?"

"A delivery of dry cleaning. Edna knew the guy by name."

"She's been with me for years, Carol, and she knows everyone that has anything to do with the house. The gardener, for instance — Edna hired him ten years ago."

Carol found herself automatically checking the garden for oleander, poinsettia and daisies. *He couldn't have taken the plants from Madeline's own garden, could he?*

"Do you have any houseplants?" she asked Madeline. "I don't think I've noticed any inside."

"Not a one. Why?" Madeline's expression changed as she realized the significance of the question. "You can't think he got the poisonous leaves here?" She gave a shaky laugh as she gestured toward the greenery in the garden. "You strike out over this theory, darling. No oleanders or poinsettias at all."

"I've already asked Edna this, but have you had anyone strange around the house in the last six months? Someone fixing something, a new plumber, electrician — anyone like that?"

"Not that I can think of. Edna organizes any repairs, and she always uses the same people."

Carol took out her notebook. "Okay, I want us to make a list of anyone who could conceivably be Marquis. It doesn't have to be a person you know well, but it's almost certain to be someone you've met. Once they've fixed on a target, stranger stalkers will often go out of their way to have some casual contact." She flipped to a clean page and unscrewed the cap of her pen. "Or, of course, it could be someone you know very well, although his claim that he saw you every day doesn't have to be true. If it is a man you socialize with, or someone at work, the real thrill for him will come from fooling you and everyone else around you."

Carol took Madeline through the staff of *The Shipley Report,* asking her if anyone had said or acted inappropriately, or if she had had serious conflict with any person who might continue to bear a grudge against her. When that drew a blank, Carol said, "How about Jim Borlie?"

"Jim? I went to school with him!" She paused,

thoughtful. "Of course, I haven't seen him for years, and people change..." She shook her head. "No, I can't believe it. Jim has never said or done anything that would make me think he could hurt me."

"Eddie Parsons ran a check on him after the attack. I won't know how accurate it is until Mark gets back to me, but there are a couple of things that might be significant."

"Are you going to tell me what they are?"

"Not unless I have a reason to. Now, how well do you know Eddie Parsons?"

"Hardly at all. I don't remember ever seeing him at the station, but I do recall he was at Tala's one time when I was there. Something about their burglar alarm. I think Gordon had sent him as a favor to Tala."

"How about Gordon Vaughan?"

"Come on!" Madeline gave an incredulous laugh. "Can you really imagine Gordon stalking me? You might as well say it's Hayden."

"He could be a possibility."

"Carol, you're having me on! Why not pick on Nevile, or even Josh Orlando?"

Edna came out of the house. Her face was white. Madeline got to her feet. "Edna? What's wrong?"

Edna tried to look impassive, but her mouth trembled. "I was moving the hangers so I could put your dry cleaning away, and I found..." She took a deep breath. "Someone's been through and slashed all your clothes. Slashed them all to pieces."

CHAPTER NINE

I've been thinking of new ways to punish you, my Madeline. I was intending to cut you in pieces, like your clothes. Then I thought, why not put out your eyes, gouge them out and squeeze the jelly between my fingers?

I've reconsidered. I want you to see me. To watch me.

Now I've decided to take a heated screwdriver and punch out your eardrums. Smash those tiny little bones inside your middle ear. They have charming names: hammer, anvil and stirrup.

The last thing you'll hear is my voice. My loving voice.

Perhaps it won't be completely silent. It seems to me you might still hear something through the beautiful bones of your skull. Your own shrieks, Madeline.

Always your Marquis

Carol was standing in the corner of Madeline's bedroom watching a member of the crime scene team dust for fingerprints when Mark Bourke arrived wearing gray Adidas sweats. "I'm supposed to be playing tennis right now. Pat and I are in the grade finals, and she's not very happy with this Marquis guy for messing up our chance at the title." He glanced at the technician. "There aren't going to be any fingerprints. We both know that."

A second person was carefully packing Madeline's ruined clothes in plastic bags. Bourke examined a wine-red dress that had been reduced to strips of frayed material. "He's losing control here — a very strong sexual component. Next could be rape, or worse."

"When he finished slashing her clothes, he tucked this letter into a jacket pocket." Carol handed him a typed page protected by a plastic sleeve.

Bourke scanned it. "Nasty. I hope Madeline or her housekeeper don't plan to stay here at the house. To say the least, it wouldn't be safe."

"Edna's in her flat out the back, packing to move to her sister's place, and Madeline's already left for a hotel."

Carol was still burning with the cold rage she had felt when they had followed Edna to the bedroom.

Carol had been silent, but Madeline had tried to make light of the situation. "Thank heavens some of my best things were at the dry cleaners," she'd said calmly, although her face had been ashen.

Bourke said soberly, "I hope the hotel's secure. I don't need to tell you this guy is very dangerous."

Carol smiled slightly. "She chose one that specializes in rock stars and their entourages, working on the theory that they would be sure to have good security."

He peered into the walk-in wardrobe. "How did he get in?"

"I'll show you." She led him down the hall to a guest bedroom. Indicating the window, she said, "A simple catch that was easy to force — a child could get in. And you can see there was cover provided by that line of bushes along the wall. No footprints — the ground's too hard. He may have broken in while Edna was at the hospital. She collected some clothes to take to Madeline late yesterday afternoon, and everything was okay then. Unfortunately Edna's a little deaf, so it's also possible he got in while she was actually here."

Bourke's mouth tightened. "Not a nice thought, to have a psycho like Marquis roaming around the house." He sat on the edge of the bed. "We've got to hope it's someone Madeline actually knows, so we can do some serious work on alibis. This guy could kill, next time."

"Sorry about the tennis, Mark, but I want you to get on to that right away." She sighed. "I'm going to leave Tom Brewer on this case, reluctant though I am, because we can't cover this and the Orlando investigation with just the two of us, and there's no one else available at the moment. Give Brewer anything you can, but keep him away from witnesses if at all possible."

"I quite look forward to upsetting Brewer's weekend plans." Bourke grinned.

As they walked back to Madeline's room he said, "By the way, have you noticed how Eddie Parsons' name seems to crop up? He arranged the installation of the security system at Tala Orlando's house, and Vaughan has told him to install a similar system here for Madeline. And isn't it interesting that Parsons is the one who asks you if you can see a link between Tala's death and Madeline's poisoning?"

"What do we know about him?"

"He's worked for Gordon Vaughan for some years. In fact, Parsons has followed him whenever Vaughan has changed jobs."

"Any record?"

"Minor stuff. Parsons has been in trouble a couple of times, mainly strong-arming when he was acting as a bodyguard. One assault conviction six years ago with a suspended sentence. That's all I've got so far. I'll put Brewer onto it and see what he can sniff out."

They stood to one side as Madeline's slashed clothes were taken out to a van to be transported to the lab.

"One thing about Parsons," said Bourke, "does impress me. That info he gave you on Jim Borlie is spot on, even the stuff about the X-rated videos. It's wonderful what you can do with a computer these days — Borlie belongs to an erotic video club and uses a credit card to pay for the selection of choice titles he has mailed to him every month."

"Parsons said Borlie had been hospitalized for mental illness."

"Two episodes of extreme depression. Nothing violent."

Violent. Marquis was violent. And his malignant hatred would be expressed more and more savagely, until he was stopped.

Carol met Ruby and Rex Courtold at the front gate of their house at Bondi Beach. They each had two black Scotch terriers on leads, and were obviously about to set out on a walk.

"I'm so sorry I'm late for our appointment," said Carol, "but something unexpected happened. I should have called..." She bent to pat the four little black dogs, who were gravely sniffing her shoes. "What beautiful Scotties."

Ruby beamed at her. "Aren't they? They're our children, you know." She pointed to each in turn. "This is Whiskey, and Jock, and Angus. And this is our youngest, Ian."

Carol smiled at Ruby Courtold's familiar face. How often on television had she seen those blue eyes, still vivid in color, and that fly-away, fine hair, once brassy blonde, but now a faded honey. Rex and Ruby had had one beloved child, a precocious son who had been found dead at nineteen in the restroom of a sleazy Kings Cross restaurant with a needle still in his arm.

"We can't go back inside, you see," said her husband, "because our boys are expecting their walk. We're going along to Marks Park, if you'd like to join us." Rex Courtold was equally familiar to Carol. He was grayer, balder, thinner, but he retained the distinctive voice and the mobile eyebrows that she remembered from countless variety shows.

"I'd be delighted. It's a beautiful day."

As they walked they chatted about Bondi Beach and the changes that the Courtolds had seen over the many years they had lived there. "The tourist buses!" said Ruby. "Everyone wants to see Bondi — it's world famous." Her tone made it obvious she was proud of her beach's international name.

The park was on a small headland jutting into the ocean. To their left was the golden curve of Bondi Beach, dotted with umbrellas and sunbathers freshening their tans before winter descended. To their right was Tamarama Bay, its discreet beach hidden by the curve of the shore. A soft breeze blew from the water, and seagulls and pigeons paced the grass competing for treats from people enjoying the sunshine.

They found a seat and the four square dogs were set free. "They're very good," Rex assured Carol. "They just sniff around."

Carol had to smile at the Scotties' bearded black faces. They were like solemn little old men who viewed life very seriously indeed. Watching them explore, she realized how reluctant she was to bring darkness into the bright day. With an inward sigh, she said, "I want to ask you about that last dinner party with Tala Orlando."

"But your Mr. Bourke has already seen us about it, Inspector," said Ruby. "Hasn't he, Rex?"

"I know that, but I'd like you to go over it again." They both gazed at her blankly. She said deliberately, "You didn't mention that Tala and her sister had a serious disagreement."

Ruby clasped her husband's hand. "But that was all patched up, so there was no reason to say anything about it."

"Please tell me everything that happened," said Carol persuasively. "It may help me understand Ms. Orlando's death."

Ruby seemed to shrink a little. "Oh, poor Tala," she said.

They took it in turns to fill in the details. They had arrived at the house at seven-thirty, walking in with Madeline and Gordon Vaughan, who had come together in one car. When their hosts greeted them, Hayden was as attentively jovial as usual, but Tala was very quiet. They were having cocktails when Tala's assistant arrived, and shortly thereafter, Robynne had let herself in.

"Robynne has her own key?" Carol interrupted.

Rex raised his expressive eyebrows. "She must have — the lounge room's near the front of the house and I heard her use it in the lock."

Rex and Ruby agreed that Tala had virtually ignored her sister, but had then abruptly asked Robynne to come with her when she went to check things in the kitchen. "I was going to the bathroom," said Ruby, "when I heard them arguing. Tala was very angry. I've never heard her talk that way to Robynne before."

"What was she saying?"

Ruby smiled apologetically at Carol. "I thought it was rude to listen. I mean, they would have both been embarrassed to know I'd overhead them."

"Do you have any idea what was making Tala angry?"

"I did hear one thing." Ruby looked ashamed, as though she had been caught deliberately eavesdropping. "Tala usually had such a soft voice, but that night she came close to yelling at Robynne. I think I can remember the exact words. Tala said, 'And all this time I thought it was Nevile, and it was *you!*' "

"We've talked about it," Rex intervened. "And we can't think what Tala meant."

Side by side, hands linked, they looked earnestly at Carol. One of the Scotch terriers flung himself down and rested his chin on Carol's foot. She absently scratched his head. "You didn't hear anything else?"

Ruby brightened. "Have you asked that girl who works for Tala?"

"Deena Bush."

"Yes. She was coming out of the bathroom just as I got there. She *must* have heard what was going on."

"I've spoken with her." Carol didn't add that Deena Bush had said she'd heard Tala and Robynne's furious voices, but that she had no idea what they'd been arguing about.

"What happened next?"

"Well, I have to admit I was curious," said Ruby with an abashed smile. "Hayden went to look for them when they didn't return, then *he* stayed away for a while. When the three of them came back, everything seemed to have calmed down."

The Scottie butted his head against Carol's hand, then rolled over to present his stomach to her. "That's Angus," said Rex proudly. "He's rather demanding."

Obediently rubbing Angus's solid little abdomen, Carol said, "You said it was all patched up, that's why you didn't mention it."

"Well, you know . . ." Ruby gestured helplessly. "It couldn't have made any difference, and it must be dreadful for Robynne to remember that last night she saw her sister they fought with each other. Rex agreed with me. It would only cause trouble."

"Did it ever occur to you that Robynne Orlando might have something to do with her sister's death?"

Carol's bald question galvanized Ruby. "Oh, no!" she said, shaking her head violently. "Robynne *loved* Tala! And there was nothing Tala wouldn't do for *her*. Robynne would never hurt her. Never!"

Carol pushed the button next to Kimberley Blackland's name. "Ms. Blackland? This is Inspector Carol Ashton. I'm sorry to disturb you on a Saturday, but I wonder if I can come up and see you?"

When the buzzer sounded, Carol pushed open the heavy glass doors guarding the affluent lobby of the apartment building. Carol had the impression that

Kimberley spent a fortune on clothes and grooming, so she must be doing well to afford this standard of accommodation as well.

Kimberley looked as though she was about to be photographed. Her makeup was perfect, her abundant hair was tamed, and she was wearing an expensive blue cashmere sweater and tailored dark slacks. "What do you want to see me about?" she asked.

"Just a few questions to clear up a couple of points." Carol looked around the room, which was a harmony of muted colors and the clean lines of graceful furniture. Several plants with large variegated leaves stood in delicately hand-painted ceramic pots. "This is lovely."

"Thank you." It was obvious Carol's appreciative remark had pleased her. "I did it all myself." She indicated the open doors. "Would you like to sit out on the balcony? It's not at all cold."

The balcony was not only small, but crowded with ornamental plants. There was a circular deep green table and matching chairs with green and blue tartan cushions. Kimberley sat forward, her elbows on the metal table. "Yes, Inspector?"

Carol watched her closely as she said, "I've just come from Madeline Shipley's house. While she was in hospital someone broke in and slashed a wardrobe full of her clothes."

Kimberley looked aghast. "How dreadful!" She frowned. "Why are you telling *me*? You can't think I had anything to do with it."

"I was wondering if you could think of anyone who might be capable of doing something like this."

She shook her head slowly. "No one. It's so

pointless and vicious. I can't imagine . . ." She looked at Carol with wide eyes. "It's the same one, isn't it? That nut that poisoned Madeline?"

"Possibly. We're still pursuing our inquiries."

"Is that all you wanted?" Kimberley appeared relieved. "I'm sorry I couldn't be more help."

"There is something else. I'm afraid I sometimes have to ask personal questions that normally would be none of my business." Carol had the appropriate measure of regret in her voice. "For example, I gather you and Gordon Vaughan have rather more than just a work relationship."

"We're friends." When Carol didn't respond, she added with a trace of defiance, "He isn't married."

According to the gossip Bourke had picked up at Channel Thirteen, although Gordon Vaughan had only been at the station a short time he had already earned a reputation for short-lived affairs. Bourke had repeated one older woman's disapproving comment, "He goes through the girls like a hot knife through butter."

Carol smiled at Kimberley. "So you're dating?"

"Sort of." Kimberley played with the large fleshy leaf of one of the potted plants. "We do see other people . . ."

"And one of those would be Joshua Orlando? You seemed close at the funeral yesterday."

Kimberley tore off a section of leaf and rolled it between her palms. "I've been out with Josh a couple of times. It's no big deal."

"And Gordon Vaughan doesn't mind?"

"Of course not." She ripped off the rest of the leaf and began to shred it. Intent upon its destruction, she said in an offhand tone, "Like I said, Gordon's a friend. We're not serious about each other."

"Who *is* he serious about?" Carol probed.

Kimberley's hands stilled. She stared levelly at Carol. "I don't know what you mean."

It was worth a bluff. Carol said, "I think you do."

Kimberley's mouth twisted. "Why don't you ask Madeline? She'd know all about it."

"I'm asking you."

"It's a surprise to me *everyone* didn't know," said Kimberley with a bitter smile. Carol waited. Kimberley continued resentfully, "I mean, Tala was always calling him, or dropping in to see him."

Hiding her surprise, Carol said, "Tala Orlando was having a relationship with Gordon Vaughan? Are you sure?"

Kimberley narrowed her eyes. "I followed them. I'm *very* sure."

"Who is it?"

Carol smiled into the peephole in the hotel room door. "Very good. You have to check absolutely everyone."

Madeline threw open the door. She was wearing a scarlet pullover and tight white jeans that she'd retrieved from the dry cleaning delivery. "Where have you been? I'm showered, I've shaved my legs — I'm all ready for you. I thought you'd come straight here after you finished at the house."

Carol's heart lurched with affection and desire.

She said, "I've been working. I've just come from Kimberley Blackland."

"Surely you don't think *she* would slash my clothes."

"She wants your job."

"Not that much!"

There was a soft knock at the door. Carol was immediately alert.

"I've ordered champagne," said Madeline as she went to the door. "And yes, I'll check it really is room service."

"Ask them to leave it outside. Say you'll sign for it later." When Madeline looked puzzled, Carol added, "It's a perfect way to get into a hotel room without arousing any suspicions. Then it's too late."

Madeline followed her instructions meekly. Carol made her wait several minutes before collecting the tray from outside the room. "Always look both ways, and be ready to slam the door if someone approaches. Treat all hotel staff as potential hazards, particularly someone like a waiter or a maid, who doesn't need an excuse to come to your room."

Watching the line of bubbles rise in her glass, Carol wondered what Tala Orlando had been celebrating with champagne the day that she died.

Madeline broke into her thoughts with a light, "Shall we drink to us, darling?" As they clinked glasses, Madeline's expression became somber. "Perhaps we should be drinking to the end of Marquis." She put down her glass and stepped forward to lean against Carol. "I'm frightened." She gave a self-deprecatory laugh. "Terrified, actually."

Carol put down her glass so she could hold her.

"You'll be safe as long as you're careful. It'll just be for a while. He'll make a mistake and we'll catch him."

"Promise?"

"I promise I'll do everything I can."

Madeline tilted her head to look up at Carol's face. Her gray eyes were wide, her mouth inviting. "Did you know fear is the ultimate aphrodisiac, Carol? It's well-documented that in life-threatening situations perfect strangers will fall upon each other and make love."

"We're not perfect strangers."

A long, slow kiss. The trembling began deep within Carol. She wanted to forget all the tensions and failures of her life. To just live for this moment, to accept what Madeline had to offer, even if there were unspoken conditions attached.

Madeline's mouth was velvet. Carol explored her teeth, her tongue, the warmth of her. When she broke the kiss, Madeline said, "Don't stop." Her voice was a throaty purr.

Suddenly exultant, Carol said, "This time I'm in charge. Tell me you'll do anything I say."

"Anything."

She put her mouth back to Madeline's and kissed her again, softly, delicately. All the time in the world. She lifted her head and Madeline protested. Carol avoided her willing mouth. "Take off your jeans," she said.

The sound of the zipper sent a thrill through her. She could hear the rasp of her own breathing. "Unbutton my shirt," she said against Madeline's lips. "Slowly, carefully. Then I'll kiss you again."

The tremor in Madeline's hands was electrifying,

sending fire to burn her thighs and tighten her stomach. She stood barely restrained as Madeline eased off her rose shirt, then ran her hands up Carol's back to undo her bra.

She pulled Madeline against her, all gentleness gone. Her bare nipples brushed against Madeline's scarlet pullover, intensifying the delicious pain between her legs.

This time Madeline drew back. "Let's get down to business." Her laugh was thick with passion.

"Not yet."

Madeline was wearing nothing under the scarlet wool. Her skin was feverishly, incandescently hot. Carol felt she could drown the past, the present, the future in Madeline's kisses, in her eager body.

"You're still half-dressed, Carol." Madeline was breathless. She undid Carol's pants and helped her step out of them. "You're wet, my darling, aren't you? Let me slide my fingers into you. Deep into you."

Her words sent a wave of stinging heat washing over Carol. Madeline was the only one who she had ever let control her, play with her. "Not this time," she whispered. "This time you're mine. On your knees."

Laughing, Madeline obediently sank down to the thick carpet. "Sit on your heels," Carol said.

Carol knelt too, cupping Madeline's full breasts in her palms, shaking so much her teeth were chattering.

"Let me," Madeline breathed. She leaned forward to take a nipple between her teeth, her tongue dancing a tattoo against the very tip. Carol threw back her head, surrendering to sensation.

With her breast held in the compulsive warmth of Madeline's mouth, Carol put one arm around her shoulders to pull her hard against her. Carol caressed her buttocks, then slipped a hand between Madeline's legs.

Madeline was hot, wet, pulsing against her urgent fingers. Her husky growl, "Yes, darling. Yes!" detonated Carol. She could no longer defy the urging of her body. When Madeline's hand assailed her, she didn't resist.

Braced together, straining, taut, unbearable.

And then — the edge reached. Tipping over.

Carol's body had eclipsed reality. Colors burst against her closed eyelids. She shuddered, bucked, pitched.

Madeline's voice purred in her ear. "Oh, darling. That was nice."

Nice? Carol listened to the sobbing of her breath. She would die to feel that way again.

CHAPTER TEN

On Sunday morning Carol left an outraged Aunt Sarah — "I was expecting to spend at least *some* time with you!" — and met Bourke in her office.

"You've been busy," he said as he surveyed the whiteboard covered with Carol's awkward block printing.

"I can never do it as neatly as you, Mark."

Bourke picked up a marker. "So what's the status on Tala Orlando?"

"Officially we're still treating it as a suspicious

death. Unofficially I'm almost convinced she was murdered."

Carol had listed the possible suspects together with notes on motive and opportunity. Bourke contributed his findings, then stood back with a look of achievement. "There you are, Carol."

Together they ran through the list. Hayden Delray had been overshadowed by his wife, both creatively and financially. Her death had given him control of Orlandel. She had died between eleven and two, and during that time her husband had been out of his office on various appointments, all within easy driving distance of the house.

For Joshua Orlando, Carol had entered a motive of financial gain. His mother had reduced his allowance and he was almost certainly unaware that she had added a condition to her will to prevent him from inheriting immediately.

"Joshua's changed his story about where he was," said Bourke. "First he claimed he was at university attending lectures, but when I investigated I found he had cut classes the day his mother died. Now he says he was with friends smoking dope, and didn't say so before because he was afraid he'd be arrested."

"Any corroboration?"

Bourke grinned. "Vague, Carol, very vague. His friends *think* he was there all the time, but the combination of cannabis and cheap red wine does impair the judgment."

Carol had noted Robynne Orlando's principal motive as money. She had been totally dependent upon her sister's generosity. The title to the house she lived in was in Tala's name, and Robynne's job with Orlandel was basically a token position.

"She wouldn't have wanted to fall out of favor," said Bourke. "If she did, she'd be up the financial creek without a paddle."

Robynne had spent the day alone next door. She had a key for easy access and ample time.

"I like Nevile Carson as the murderer," said Bourke. "He has every reason to hate Tala because not only does she throw him out of Orlandel, but also, if he's to be believed, she stole his idea for a hit quiz show."

"He may be telling the truth about the offer to settle from Tala. She'd be quite capable of making it without bothering to consult with her husband."

Bourke tapped the marker against Carson's name. "Don't defend my prime suspect, please. I like it that he hasn't really got an alibi. He certainly checked in his luggage in the morning, then took the delayed flight to Perth when it left in the afternoon, but there's nothing to prove he stayed at the airport, as he claimed. He could just as easily have left to drive to Tala's house."

Carol said, "You've double-checked all Tala's neighbors, haven't you?"

Bourke spread his hands. "Every last one, with exactly the same result as the first sweep. Those few who were home during the day saw nothing, heard nothing, and didn't notice any strange cars or people. This isn't surprising when you see how privacy is at a premium in the area and most of the houses are set well back from the road."

Carol pointed to the final two names she'd added to the column of suspects. "Gordon Vaughan is there because of Kimberley Blackland's unsupported word that he and Tala were having an affair. And

Kimberley makes the list for the same reason, although it seems unlikely she'd deliberately set out to make herself a suspect by providing a motive we knew nothing about. We need to know if there's any truth in what she says, not least because it gives Hayden Delray another motive. I want you to give it priority tomorrow."

Bourke rolled his eyes. "I'll add it to my long list of things to do." He surveyed the names on the board. "You know, the crucial time seems to be between one and two in the afternoon, since the cleaner was in the house until one o'clock."

Carol demurred. "Tala may have already been dead. The internal entrance to the garage can't be seen from the kitchen or dining room, the areas where Isabel was working. Don't forget that someone intending to kill her can enter through the main garage door and meet her there — it isn't necessary to go through the front door into the house. Perhaps she *had* opened the garage and was ready to drive out when she was intercepted."

"Unlikely, Carol. In your scenario Tala obligingly washes down a fair dose of tranquilizers with champagne, then, conveniently woozy, she wanders down to the garage to meet her murderer. And through all this, Isabel Snipes-More cleans on, oblivious. I can't buy that."

"What if there's an accomplice? One person to drug her and one to kill her?"

"Now you're getting complicated," said Bourke.

When Carol called Nevile Carson he seemed

genuinely pleased to hear from her. "I was just planning to walk down to Balmoral to have coffee and croissants. Why don't you join me there?"

Carol had trouble parking. It was always difficult during the weekend, but the beautiful day had brought even larger numbers to the harbor beach. The yellow sand was crowded and a constant stream of people strolled along the esplanade. Finally she saw the welcome flash of reversing lights and slid into the spot as soon as the car backed out of the angle-parking.

Beside the old bathing pavilion, now converted to a restaurant, members of an art group were self-consciously working at canvases under instruction from a bearded, paint-stained teacher. Carol joined the people who had paused to admire their efforts. It amazed her how one person could capture with a few strokes the color and movement of the scintillating water, the texture of the sand — when someone at the next easel, using the same materials, could only produce a static and lifeless representation.

Nevile Carson was sitting at a small table he had commandeered outside the café. His thinning hair was hidden by a baseball cap and he wore shorts and a white polo shirt. "Let me treat you, Inspector, or would that be taken as an attempt at bribery?"

Carol thought again how his deep voice seemed somehow incongruous in such a lightly built man. Matching his flippant tone, she said, "I don't think one cup of coffee would corrupt me."

He looked approvingly at her black jeans and aquamarine top. "You look good in casual clothes."

"Thank you."

Carson caught the attention of a harried waiter

and gave their order. Turning back to Carol, he said, "I saw you looking at the artists' work. Do you paint?"

"I haven't an artistic bone in my body," said Carol ruefully, curious to see how long he would persevere with small talk.

"But surely solving crime is artistry in its own way." He gave her a closed-lip smile. "You start your investigation with a blank canvas, and then you fill in details until you have the whole picture. Isn't that how it is?"

"I've never heard it described quite that way."

He was watching her intently, the glare making him squint through his tortoise-shell glasses. "Regarding Tala's death — just how close are you to the whole picture?"

She smiled at him. "I'm hoping you'll help by filling in a few details. The first may just be gossip."

His expression didn't change. "Go on."

"We've been told that Tala Orlando may have been having an affair with Gordon Vaughan."

"And you want my opinion?" A slight smile twitched his lips. "What makes you think I'd know anything about it?"

"You've been seeing Gordon Vaughan frequently about a sitcom you're developing. I wondered if he'd said anything that would indicate his interest in Ms. Orlando."

The waiter appeared with two coffees and a plate of croissants. Nevile Carson regarded Carol pensively as they were placed on the table. When they were alone, he said, "How very perspicacious of you, Inspector, to realize Vaughan's vanity and stupidity. He dropped enough hints for me to read between the lines. He never came out with it in so many words, but it was clear he wanted me to know that he and Tala were a great deal more than friends." He gave an almost imperceptible shrug. "I've since wondered why he felt it particularly necessary to let *me* know about them, and frankly I've decided it was just his egotism and pride. Tala was a prize he couldn't boast about, except to someone like me, who wouldn't be believed if I said anything against her."

Carol took a sip of her black coffee. "Would Vaughan's involvement with Tala make it unlikely he'd give serious consideration to your concept for a new sitcom?"

He grunted with amusement. "Of course not. That's a business decision. You don't think Gordon Vaughan's got where he is by allowing sentiment to get in the way, do you?"

"I believe you proposed Madeline Shipley as a possible lead," Carol said casually.

"Madeline's physically quite beautiful," Carson acknowledged, "but I'm not totally convinced she can act. I say that because it wasn't me who suggested she might be cast in the main role. I talked to her about it, but it was Vaughan's idea." He paused. "I believe he has an interest in Madeline, if you know what I mean."

He leaned over to feed a piece of croissant to a particularly assertive seagull whose quest for scraps had taken it closer to the tables than any of its companions. "I'm fond of seagulls," he said. "I like their pushy attitude toward life."

Carol said bluntly, "Tala and her sister were overheard having a violent argument the night before Tala was found dead. Your name was mentioned."

Carson sat back in his chair. "Indeed? Not favorably, I imagine."

"Apparently Tala said to your ex-wife something like, 'All the time I thought it was Nevile, and it was *you.*' Would you have any idea what she meant by that?"

"Of course I know." His face was quite expressionless. "It took a long time, but Tala had finally realized what Robynne was really like."

"And that was . . . ?"

"You must know, Inspector, that the best defense is very often attack. Two years ago, when Robynne thought she was about to be caught out, she turned around and accused me of all the things she had actually done herself." He clasped his thin hands on the table and continued evenly, "I didn't know it at that stage, but Robynne had been selling information about Orlandel's projects to our competitors for some time. Our marriage was already in trouble, so it must have seemed to her to be an excellent way to get rid of me and stay in favor with Tala at the same time."

"But surely," said Carol, "you presented your side of the story."

"If you were Tala, Inspector, who would you want to believe had betrayed you? Your beloved sister? Or your brother-in-law?" He cocked his head. "Not a hard question, is it? It was a walk-over for Robynne."

Madeline hooted when Carol called her at the hotel to repeat Nevile Carson's contention that Gordon Vaughan was interested in her. "Gordon? I don't think so. Sometimes we partner each other on social occasions, and may even do a bit of ritual flirting, but that doesn't mean a thing. Besides, I'm sure he knows about us."

"You're out of the closet for Gordon Vaughan?"

"Give it a rest, Carol!" Madeline snapped, responding to Carol's sarcastic tone.

Carol suddenly had the disagreeable thought that this was exactly what Sybil had complained about for so long about *her.* Carol had finally refused to discuss the subject at all — she had intended to stay in the closet whether Sybil liked it or not.

Circumstances had changed the situation completely. However reluctantly, Carol was now out. And now Madeline was playing Carol's previous role, wanting everything from Carol except public acknowledgment of their relationship.

Carol's silence brought a plaintive response from Madeline. "I'm sorry. Don't punish me by saying you won't see me tonight."

"Aunt Sarah's staying with me for the weekend. I haven't seen her all day and I promised her we'd go out to dinner."

"After that? I don't care how late you are." Madeline's voice dropped to a whispered invitation. "You know I can make it worth your while."

Perversely irritated that even an obliquely provocative comment from Madeline could incite a flutter of desire, Carol said briskly, "Don't wait up for me. If I'm not too late, I'll call, but don't rely on me coming."

Madeline gave a low laugh. "But darling, that's one thing I *can* rely on."

* * * * *

Her aunt was talkative on the way home from the local Greek restaurant. "Do you mind if I stay a couple more days? I've got some shopping to do, and Esther Thorpe — she was my bridesmaid forty-five years ago — is having a bridge party on Tuesday."

"You know you can stay as long as you like. Jeffrey and Sinker really appreciate the attention."

"So should you, Carol," Aunt Sarah said bracingly. "It isn't good for you to live alone. You become too set in your ways."

Carol swung into the street-level carport beside her aunt's disreputable brown station wagon. "I'm perfectly happy by myself."

"Rubbish!" Her aunt punctuated this by slamming the car door with vigor. "You won't admit it, but you're lonely."

Carol stopped so abruptly on the narrow path leading to the front door that Aunt Sarah bumped into her. "Carol, what are you doing?"

"Something's wrong." The hair prickled on the back of her neck. The moonlight was confusing, creating a silver and black world where threats hid in every shadow.

Aunt Sarah peered over her shoulder. "The light over the front door is out. The globe's probably blown."

"I left a light on in the house. That's off too." Carol slid her hand into her shoulder bag and closed her palm around the comforting cold metal of her gun. She could feel her pulse thudding in her throat. "The front door's open," she said softly. "Someone's been here — they may still be. I'm not taking any chances. I want you to go back to the street and knock on my next door neighbor's front door. Call the police."

"I'm not leaving you alone, Carol. You've armed, aren't you?"

"Aunt, I'm asking you to go."

"No way," Aunt Sarah snorted. "Besides, I might be ambushed. *Then* what would you do?"

Carol took her weapon out. "I haven't time to argue."

Her aunt nudged her in the back. "I'll keep right behind you, dear. I've got to make sure the cats are okay."

The cats. Carol had a nightmare vision of what might have happened to them. It could be a simple break-in, but if it were Marquis he wasn't likely to have scruples about hurting little animals.

"Keep close, Aunt Sarah. The fuse box is on the wall down the side of the house. He's almost certainly turned off the power at the main switch."

Although she felt certain that if it was Marquis there'd be no incriminating fingerprints, Carol opened the metal cabinet with care and flipped the switch back on with the butt of her gun. Light flared at the front of the house. There was a rustle in the garden, and she swung around, automatically assuming firing stance, her forefinger sliding from its safety position along the guard to rest on the trigger.

Sinker wound his black and white body around Aunt Sarah's legs, pointedly ignoring Carol. The person who fed him last always received special attention.

Aunt Sarah grabbed him and wedged him firmly under one arm. "Now where's Jeffrey? Sybil would never forgive us if something happened to him."

Clutching the wriggling cat, Aunt Sarah shadowed Carol as she circled the house, checking rooms through windows and switching on any outside lights as she went. Arriving back at the front door, Carol made her aunt wait in the garden as she edged her way inside. She could feel her heart thudding with alarm — she presented a perfect target in the open doorway. Carol wanted to believe this was just an ordinary, mundane housebreaking, but it seemed far too much of a coincidence that it should occur at the same time that Madeline was being stalked.

"You should have a burglar alarm," her aunt hissed.

Carol gestured for her to be quiet. She stood in the familiar hallway listening for any alien sound. The refrigerator hummed loudly in the silence. She could hear Sinker, still imprisoned, growl his displeasure.

Carol swiftly checked each room. "Okay, inside." The front door hadn't been forced, so Carol shut and locked it. She began an intensive search, examining every possible hiding place. There was nothing. No signs of disturbance. No typed note.

They found Jeffrey curled up in a ginger ball at the end of Carol's bed. He stretched and yawned with a wide pink mouth when the light came on. Carol was so pleased to see him that she squeezed his sleepy body against her.

Aunt Sarah had been subdued as Carol had searched the house. Once she had deposited a ruffled Sinker on the floor, she had anxiously followed Carol from room to room. Now her buoyant spirits were returning. "Well, dear," she said, "we must have frightened off whoever it was when we came home. I've checked my things, and nothing's been touched. You'd better get the locks changed, and we can forget it ever happened." She looked at the gun still in Carol's hand. "And you can put that away."

Carol picked up the phone. "I'm calling the local station to send a squad car and someone for fingerprints. The grounds have to be searched properly as well as beneath the house and the space under the roof."

This thought was an unwelcome surprise. Aunt Sarah stared at the ceiling. "Carol," she whispered, "do you really think there's a chance someone's up there *now*?"

Carol gestured with her gun. "I'm not taking any chances."

After she'd contacted the local police, she dialed Madeline's hotel.

"Darling, you *are* coming over?"

Carol briefly explained. "So I won't see you tonight. I can't leave Aunt Sarah here alone." She was struck by a sudden thought. "Who's driving you to Channel Thirteen tomorrow? Gordon Vaughan said he'd be arranging a security driver."

"Eddie Parsons called me this evening. He said he'd be taking me himself."

"I don't like that." Carol had taken the point Mark Bourke had made that morning — it was odd how Eddie Parsons linked the two cases. "Madeline, call back and cancel. I'll arrange for Mark to pick you up."

Next she called Bourke. As she was talking the

local police officers arrived. While one dusted for fingerprints, the others swept the grounds efficiently and investigated the storage area under the house. Finally a young constable clambered through the ceiling access up into the attic.

"Not a thing, Inspector," said the officer in charge. "Whoever he is, he's long gone."

She thanked them and sent them on their way. Aunt Sarah changed into a chartreuse nightgown and fluffy pink slippers and fussed around the kitchen.

"Here, dear, drink this. It'll help you sleep."

Taking the proffered mug reluctantly, Carol said, "I hate hot milk."

Aunt Sarah was implacable. "There's a chemical in milk that calms you down. I want you to drink every last drop."

Carol took a mouthful and made a face. "This tastes revolting."

Her aunt propped herself against the breakfast counter. "You don't think this was just an unsuccessful housebreaking, do you? You're afraid it's something to do with Madeline Shipley's stalker."

"Could be." Carol loathed the thought that a stranger had invaded the sanctuary of her home, touched her possessions. Or even worse, perhaps not a stranger, but somebody she knew, who masked his cold malice with normality.

She slept badly, barely comforted by the cool metallic sheen of the gun on the bedside table. Fully awake at dawn, she lay flat on her back with her hands linked behind her head, reviewing the candidates for Marquis.

Jim Borlie had been her first suspect. His job was to know Madeline's routine and keep track of her appointments. How had Eddie Parsons described Borlie? *An inadequate little bastard.* He seemed innocuous, insignificant. Did the scorn of people like Parsons, the success of people like Madeline, ignite him with hidden venom?

Eddie Parsons was on Carol's list. She disliked his smugness and self-satisfaction, but had to acknowledge that he was probably very good at his job. Although he seemed to have had no direct contact with Madeline before the poisoning, his position in charge of security gave him unquestioned access to information about her.

That brought her to Gordon Vaughan, who had had a long working relationship with Eddie Parsons. She hoped Tom Brewer's report would fill in more details, but it seemed obvious that Parsons owed Vaughan a great deal. Was it feasible that they were accomplices? Carol knew it was rare for a stalker to work with a second person, but not totally unknown.

Kimberley Blackland was also a possibility. Bourke had thought the slashing of Madeline's clothes indicated escalating sexual frenzy, but Carol wondered if it couldn't equally indicate the intensity of a consuming envy. Kimberley blazed with ambition. She coveted Madeline's position but had no chance of taking her place unless something unforeseen occurred. For Madeline to be injured or killed would be very much to Kimberley's advantage.

When she considered Eddie Parsons' suggestion that there might be a link between Tala Orlando's death and the attacks on Madeline, the list of possible suspects immediately became longer to include Hayden Delray, Nevile Carson, Joshua Orlando and even Robynne Orlando.

Carol sat up. *Or it could be a total stranger.* Exclaiming in frustration, she swung her legs over the edge of the bed and stood to stretch. She was going in circles. She had to know *why* Madeline was being stalked, however irrational the reason, before she could identify the face that concealed Marquis.

As Carol was filling her ancient percolator at the sink, Aunt Sarah came out yawning. "Going for your run, dear? I think it's a good idea, as long as you take Olga with you."

"I don't like to leave you alone."

"That sort of person doesn't turn up in broad daylight," said Aunt Sarah scornfully. "Besides, I'm a mean shot with a rifle, so I dare say I could use your gun to some effect."

"Put the security chain on the front door. I'll be about half an hour."

Olga was delighted to be going out earlier than usual. She effortlessly kept up, even though Carol was pushing herself to the limit in an effort to burn away the stress that knotted her stomach.

Comforted by the presence of the formidable German shepherd running beside her, Carol had no sense of personal danger. She knew Olga would protect her against a physical attack. But an onslaught against peace of mind was harder to circumvent.

She thought of Madeline's usual insouciant attitude toward life. However resilient, the constant threats would eventually undermine Madeline's belief that her world was essentially safe and predictable.

Carol turned for home, slowing to a comfortable, easy pace. The morning air was sharply cold, and her breath steamed. She put Olga through her neighbor's gate, then padded down the front path.

There was the same sickening hollowness as last night. This time the front door wasn't open, but there was a white rectangle attached at eye height. When she moved closer, she could read the name at the bottom of the sheet of paper. *Marquis.*

CHAPTER ELEVEN

Who do you love most in the world, Carol? Yourself? Or perhaps it's your son, David.

He's twelve, isn't he? A very bright young man. I've spoken to him, but of course David thought I was just another adult. No one special. Not someone who holds his life or death in my hands.

I watched you last night. Just as I watch David. Every little detail. I'm there when he leaves Justin Hart's house to catch the bus to school. For a barrister who sees the wicked things that happen in life, your ex-husband's a little careless, Carol. Anyone could snatch David right off the street. Into a car, and he'd be gone. Gone for good.

David wouldn't die straightaway, of course. I want you to picture him screaming, crying. Do you think he'd call out for his Mummy? Not his stepmother, his real Mummy?

Believing you could save him. Faith like that is so touching, Carol.

"Justin, it's Carol."

"Is something wrong?"

"Where's David?"

"He's just having breakfast. Why?"

"He mustn't go to school today. I've just come back from my morning run and there was something pinned to the front door. A threat to kidnap David, to hurt him. Stay there with him. I'll be right over."

"Carol, be reasonable. I've got clients who expect me to be in court. I can't stay. Eleanor's here. David will be okay with her."

"Justin, please!"

Bourke sat in Carol's office looking grimly at a copy of the note. "Where's David now?"

Carol rested her elbows on her desk, rubbing her temples where the insistent throb of a headache was beginning. "I eventually persuaded Justin this was a genuine threat. Eleanor's taking David to her brother's place. It's a sheep station in the middle of nowhere." She made an effort to sound unconcerned. "You know what it's like in the country, Mark. The moment a stranger turns up, everyone in the district knows, so I can't imagine Marquis getting a chance to snatch him there."

She could still see her son's puzzled face as she'd tried to explain why he had to go away for a few days. "But Mum, I *can't* miss any school. I'm trying out for the soccer team today . . ."

And Justin had taken her aside to say in a low, dangerous voice, "Carol, this is totally unacceptable. Why should something you do impinge on our son this way? I think we should reconsider the visitation arrangements. David shouldn't see you if it means his life is put in danger."

Carol tried to concentrate on the report Bourke had just given her detailing the financial status of Carson, Delray and Joshua Orlando, but the pages just seemed to be a series of random marks on white paper.

God, what if he hurts David? I would kill him. Kill him.

Bourke's voice brought her out of her thoughts. "We're not getting anywhere fast with Marquis. The computer check of Channel Thirteen staff didn't turn up anything startling, and as we expected, it's negative for fingerprints at Madeline's place and yours. The lab couldn't find much of interest with the slashed clothes either, except to say a very sharp blade was used and that it would have taken him some time to do it, since every item in the wardrobe was systematically attacked. As for opportunity, the time frames are so wide that it's virtually impossible to rule anyone out."

Carol fished in her top drawer for aspirin. "Headache," she said in explanation.

"Stay there. I'll get you some water."

While Bourke was gone she looked at Nevile Carson's financial profile. He wasn't in Tala Orlando's league, but he had sound property investments and was under contract to provide Channel Thirteen with program concepts for the next two years. Bourke had noted that although Carson had the money to mount a legal case against Orlandel, Tala's company had far greater financial resources to draw upon and would win a war of attrition. From Carson's point of view, a settlement that saved him legal costs and gave him some part of the profits of *Take the Risk* was an excellent proposition.

Bourke came back with a glass of water and watched her take the aspirin. "This is a double game Marquis is playing," he said. "Stalkers usually stick with one target."

Carol swallowed the last of the water. "It might be my association with Madeline. He wants her to himself and he sees me as being in the way."

"Maybe." Bourke wasn't convinced.

"Look, David's safe. That's the important thing."

Bourke looked at her soberly. "But you're not, Carol. He could hurt you. He knows where you live. He knows your routine." He sighed. "You should check your car every morning, or better still, always get a taxi."

"You seriously think he'd plant a bomb?"

"I believe you should be careful. It doesn't take an Einstein to cut brake lines, and you can't see your car from the house. Anyone could tamper with it." He touched her hand — a rare physical contact for him. "I talked it over with Pat this morning. You could stay with us."

"Thank you, but no." She was emphatic. "I'm not going to be driven out of my home. I tried to send Aunt Sarah back to the Blue Mountains, but she insisted she wouldn't leave Sydney until this was cleared up. She's at the house at the moment, supervising the local locksmith while he installs new deadlocks and burglar-proof window catches."

"You're not using Eddie Parsons?" asked Bourke mockingly. "I hear he does home security for the very best people."

She didn't smile. "Mark, the front door wasn't forced. Either someone had a key, which is very unlikely, or it was unlocked by an expert. That could be Parsons."

"If your aunt's going to stay in the house she'll have to take precautions. She could be in danger."

"I've persuaded her to move in with friends at Bilgola." With a ghost of a smile, Carol remembered the battle her aunt had put up at the suggestion of leaving Carol alone. "The ones who have the most reason to complain are Sinker and Jeffrey. Aunt Sarah will be dropping them off at a boarding kennel later today. They won't be pleased."

"Someone else who isn't pleased is Madeline," said Bourke. "When I drove her to Channel Thirteen this morning she spent most of the time telling me I had to persuade you to move into the hotel with her. You wouldn't be safe anywhere else, she said."

"I've told her no," said Carol impatiently.

He put up his hands. "I don't want to be involved." He grinned. "It's the irresistible force and the immovable object all over again."

"Give me an irresistible force any day," said Tom Brewer as, hands in pockets, he strolled through the door. He slumped into the nearest chair. "I've been working my butt off for you, Inspector." He showed his teeth in a wolfish grin. "Want me to lay it on you now?" He didn't wait for an answer, but maneuvered himself until he could extract his notebook from the hip pocket of his wrinkled brown trousers. "Let's see . . ."

Carol had decided that nothing Brewer could say or do was going to provoke her, but she felt a strong urge to make an acid comment or two. She had received his sloppily written report on the Marquis letters and had very little faith that he would do better with any other task. She glanced at Bourke, who was watching Brewer with a suspiciously solemn face.

"Typewriters and poisonous plants," said Brewer. "A big help if we can match them with the clues Marquis has obligingly left. Mind you, all the more reason to think they're red herrings." He flipped over a few pages in his notebook. "Of course Channel Thirteen uses computers, but I found a few type-writers around the place, mainly gathering dust. There were a couple being used for the odd envelope or label, but not one came close to the typeface of the letters."

"I agree with Tom," said Bourke. "It's a red herring. Marquis is not going keep a typewriter where we can find it and tie it to him. And even if he *has* got it at home, we can't do a random search without cause."

Brewer gave a pleased nod. "Couldn't put it better

myself." Chewing his gum loudly, he referred to his notes. "Marquis mentions having a particular potted plant, a leopard lily or dumb cane, in his living room. I'd say that's another red herring. So we're left with the leaves Shipley ate — oleander, daisy and poinsettia collected outside, and elephant's ear and nonstera deliciosa from houseplants." He closed his notebook and stretched out his skinny legs. "You know, it's a fascinating thing. I've always been interested in gardening, so when I prowled around both the Orlando and the Delray gardens I didn't have any trouble finding that, between the two of them, you could collect everything you needed. Plus there's an enclosed spa bath at the back of Robynne Orlando's place that has indoor plants growing like a jungle. Includes the two we want — and she even has a leopard lily."

Carol rolled her pen between her palms. "I'm hardly an expert on plants, but Kimberley Blackland has something that could be a leopard lily in her apartment."

Brewer rolled his head to ease his shoulders. "You know, if I were this Marquis guy, I'd collect a sample from a whole lot of different places — try and incriminate as many people as possible. It'd be a game."

"Have you got anything else?" asked Carol, making an effort to repress her annoyance.

Brewer went back to his notebook. "I sure have. Mark told me to check on the accident that killed Gordon Vaughan's first wife. She snuffed it three years ago when he was driving the car. Don't ask me how Vaughan managed it, but they ran off the road and into Narrabeen Lakes. Shallow water, but she drowned. *He* didn't." He beamed at Carol. "No alcohol in his blood. Suspicious, eh?"

"He wasn't charged with anything?"

"Not a thing. Just an accident." Brewer rubbed his jaw. "The best of all possible worlds, don't you think? He gets rid of his wife and remains Shearing's favorite son-in-law. I'd say Vaughan's on his way to the very top of the network, no worries."

"How about Eddie Parsons?" said Bourke. He rarely showed irritation, but Carol could see that Tom Brewer was finally getting to him.

"Eddie Parsons..." There was more flipping of pages. Brewer looked up with a grin. "My kind of bloke. He's a gun for hire who never minds getting his hands a little dirty. Happy to lean on someone for you, or collect a debt. He's done a lot for Gordon Vaughan, including being a witness at the wife's inquest. Parsons got up and testified she couldn't swim and was terrified of water. The general consensus was that she'd panicked when the car submerged, taken a lungful of water and died. Accidental death."

"Convenient," said Bourke.

"Very. And Parsons's been rewarded for it. He has a little security business on the side — installs alarms, deadlocks, that sort of thing. Vaughan makes sure that all the network business goes Eddie's way, plus he steers any friends who need a house alarm system in the same direction."

"What does Vaughan get out of this arrangement?" said Carol.

"Why, *loyalty,* Inspector." Brewer was very amused. "Absolute bloody loyalty." He snapped his notebook shut. "One more thing. The day Orlando died, Eddie wasn't at work. He took a few days off that week, for personal matters, he said. Now, I'd call that interesting."

Carol sent Bourke to see Robynne Orlando again, and then to check the motel that Kimberley claimed Vaughan and Tala Orlando had used for assignations.

With some trepidation, she told Brewer to call on Kimberley Blackland at her apartment. Carol had confidence that, if nothing else, Brewer had some skills in identifying plants, and she wanted to know if there was a leopard lily in the ornamental pots in the living room.

Carol had made appointments to see Hayden Delray and Joshua Orlando. She was hoping that by keeping busy she could ignore the gnawing anxiety about David that threatened to overcome her. She had the telephone number and had already called Eleanor's brother, only to be told that they hadn't yet arrived.

The same sleek receptionist smiled from behind the black marble counter. With every evidence of delight, she exclaimed, "Inspector Ashton! Mr. Delray is expecting you. I'll arrange for someone to take you to his office."

While she waited, Carol considered the profile Bourke had given her on Hayden Delray's financial standing. "Nothing worth mentioning of his own," Bourke had said. "Delray draws a six-figure salary, but seems to spend every red cent. When he married Tala Orlando he was running his own little production company, but it was close to bankruptcy."

"So Tala essentially controlled the money?"

"Held it in a viselike grip. Once Hayden had run through his salary, he had to ask her for money, like a kid asking for an allowance. Mind you, it seems he never complained about the setup, and Tala always gave him what he asked for."

"Inspector?" The glowing receptionist broke into her thoughts. "Deena will take you up."

Deena Bush was all awkward angles, her thin thighs barely covered by a minuscule skirt. She tugged at a strand of her honey-blonde hair. "He's waiting for you. Come this way."

Carol smiled pleasantly at her. "Have you finished clearing out Ms. Orlando's office?"

"Yeah, almost. The decorators start tomorrow."

As they reached Hayden Delray's door, Carol said, "I'll look in on you before I go."

This innocuous comment seemed to disturb Deena. She looked sideways at Carol. "All right," she said doubtfully, "but I've told you everything I know."

Hayden Delray wasn't welcoming. His face was puffy and he had dark circles under his eyes. "I have a very tight schedule, Inspector. I trust this won't take long."

He'd taken off his suit coat and rolled up his shirt sleeves. Carol noticed his heavy forearms were thick with sandy hair. He wore a large gold watch with an elaborate dial and a plain wedding band so tight that it bit into the flesh of his ring finger.

"You haven't been altogether frank with me, Mr. Delray," said Carol.

"In what way?" His ruddy skin radiated antagonism.

"Contrary to what you implied, our investigations

show that your wife and sister-in-law were in serious conflict," said Carol formally. "At issue was whether Robynne Orlando had been selling information to your company's competitors, an accusation she'd originally leveled at her ex-husband."

"Carson!" he said contemptuously. "You believe *him*? He's got an ax to grind."

"We have corroboration from another source," said Carol smoothly.

He glowered at her. "Who? Not Deena Bush? I wouldn't trust anything she said."

Carol wondered about the strength of the card she was about to play. "Would you trust Ruby Courtold?"

Delray seemed to deflate at little. "Ruby," he said. "Tala thought she'd overheard . . ."

Deena Bush jumped when Carol knocked gently on the open door. "I was just clearing out the last things," she said defensively.

Carol looked around the room, thinking how Tala's office had lost its individual style. The watercolors were gone from the walls and the cream and rose striped chairs had been removed. Deena had obviously gone through all the papers, as the desk top was now covered with miscellaneous items including a ceramic pen caddy, paper clip tray, personal stationery, an address book, several note pads and two small plastic bottles.

Carol picked one up and examined it. "What's this?"

Deena glanced at it without interest. "Just some herbal stuff she took."

Carol unscrewed the top and tipped out the pills onto her palm. "I thought Ms. Orlando wouldn't take any drugs."

"She wouldn't. This was natural stuff from a health food store. She took them every morning. Never missed."

The second canister held gelatin capsules with a gray powder inside. The label declared, *Organic Garlic Special Formula.*

"Are there any more of these?"

Deena scrabbled around in a desk drawer and found two more containers. Scribbling a receipt on one of the note pads, Carol said, "I'm taking these, okay?"

Deena raised her thin shoulders. "I don't care. I was going to throw them out."

While she drove to her appointment with Joshua Orlando, Carol reviewed the discussion she'd had about him with Bourke. "Joshua's failing his courses badly," Mark had said. "Spends most of his time at the gym bulking up, or hanging around with friends doing nothing in particular. Unless he does a great deal better in his exams at the end of this semester, the university will throw Joshua out on his ear. His mother gave him a very generous allowance until his results started sliding, then Tala wasn't amused and cut the money until he could show her he was going to apply himself."

"So financially he's in trouble?"

"At the moment, yes. He lives with friends in a flat near the university, which doesn't cost much, but he drives a Porsche that his mother bought him for his twentieth birthday, and he's developed expensive tastes to match his car."

"Any romantic interests?"

"Kimberley Blackland's dated him a couple of times." Bourke had put on a lofty expression. "I'm a modern man. I approve of younger men and older women."

"What did Tala think?"

"I've no idea, but Aunt Robynne approved. Apparently she encouraged Joshua to date Kimberley in the first place."

Joshua Orlando had moved back to his student flat, and Carol found the inner city address without difficulty. It was on Glebe Point Road, a refurbished terrace house that had once been elegant, but had become a victim of clumsy modernization. He shared a flat at the back, and Carol was let in by a young woman with an intense, ugly-beautiful face.

Joshua, barefoot and wearing a tight sleeveless T-shirt and shabby jeans, was lounging on a brightly covered floral sofa. Although he got up without haste to greet Carol, his pale blue eyes were alert. "I can't imagine what else I can possibly tell you, Inspector Ashton." He was fully a head shorter than Carol, and had to tilt his chin to meet her eyes. He grunted. "I suppose you'd better sit down."

Carol had to remind herself that this was the son of a woman who had died only a few days ago in tragic circumstances. If he was grieving, there was no outward sign.

"It's only a couple of things," she said reassuringly. "We have new information that sheds light on the message your mother left on your answering machine."

"What sort of information?" he said curtly.

"I've just seen Hayden Delray."

Joshua put his hands behind his head, the movement rippling the heavily developed muscles of his chest. "So? My stepfather has never liked me, Inspector. And he likes me a lot less now I've got a share of Orlandel. It's a mistake to believe anything he says about me."

"Where did you get the information about your Aunt Robynne?"

He abandoned his nonchalant pose. Sitting forward on the sofa, he said with a faintly puzzled air, "I'm not sure I know what you mean."

"No?" Carol raised her eyebrows. "Mr. Delray says you approached him and told him that Robynne Orlando had been selling information about Orlandel's future projects to other companies. You had some specific examples."

"And you believe him?" said Joshua indignantly.

"Why would he lie?"

Joshua gestured angrily. "I don't know!"

"As you can see," said Carol reasonably, "this would make the meaning of your mother's message clear. If Mr. Delray has repeated to her what you've told him, then it makes sense for her to say that it's difficult for her, but she can't ignore the accusation — she has to do something about it."

"I didn't say a thing to him about my aunt. It's his word against mine."

Carol was persistent. "Who would know enough to give you that information? Nevile Carson, perhaps?"

He blinked. "Carson? The funeral on Friday was the first time I'd seen him for ages." He frowned at her. "Look, you've got it wrong. I didn't say anything to anybody."

Carol persevered, but he remained obdurate. As he was showing her out the door, she said casually, "You've been going out with Kimberley Blackland."

He gave a snort of derisive laughter. "I was, until I realized she was just working the angles. She's already sweet-talked Aunt Robynne, and Kimberley thought dating me would definitely be the thing to get her in good with my mother."

"Did it work?"

"Get real! Mum was the one who told me to drop her."

Carol had just broken the connection to David, who had arrived safely at the country property, when Bourke called her on the car phone. "Carol, something you'll be fascinated to hear. The delightful Isabel Snipes-More wasn't in Tala's house from nine to one that day, no matter what she said in her statement."

A gap in the traffic to the right opened up, and Carol quickly cut in. "How do you know?"

He chuckled. "Blame my charm ... or Robynne Orlando's conscience. Robynne says she didn't mention it before because she was too embarrassed to admit she'd been cheating her sister. It seems Isabel was in the habit of dropping in to see Robynne when cleaning Tala's house next door. Isabel would do some chore for Robynne — say, washing — and charge the time to Tala. Robynne was getting something for nothing, and as Isabel inflated her hours as a matter of course, this removed the worry that Robynne would notice what was going on and tell her sister."

Carol edged over another lane, then braked for a red light. "Bottom line, Mark."

"The times? I'm off right now to see Isabel herself, but Robynne tells me that she came in about eleven-thirty, cleaned some silver for about half an hour, then split."

"Isabel must have been sure Tala had left the house before she left early."

"She told Robynne that she called out, and when Tala didn't answer, Isabel just assumed she'd gone down to her car and driven off to work." He added enthusiastically, "Since the earliest Tala could have died is eleven, it seems to me this narrows the time of death considerably."

"Have you considered the possibility," said Carol, "that Tala did leave, just as Isabel thought, but came back later?"

Bourke groaned. "You always rain on my parade."

CHAPTER TWELVE

While they waited for a red light to change, Bourke examined a bit of skin from his sunburnt nose. "I'm falling to pieces," he said dolefully.

"Yeah, mate," said Brewer from the back seat. "We all are."

The late afternoon traffic was heavy. Carol was tired and impatient, inwardly chaffing at their stop-start progress. Mark Bourke had come back to her office with two salient pieces of information: first, Isabel Snipes-More confirmed the times Robynne had given him and also admitted that she had forgotten to set the security alarm when she left the house; second, the motel desk clerk had turned up payment records to show that a double room had been rented on several occasions to Channel Thirteen and signed for by Gordon Vaughan. Now she wanted to confront him and get the truth. She thought of Nevile Carson's description of an evolving investigation as a painting. How many brushstrokes would be needed before the shadowy figure in the center was revealed?

Carol sighed as the traffic again ground to a halt. Turning around in her seat, she said to Brewer, "When we get to Channel Thirteen, Mark will be meeting Jim Borlie and then Kimberley Blackland while you and I see Gordon Vaughan. Have you got it straight how we'll run the interview?"

"Got it straight." Brewer grinned at her mockingly. He adjusted the knot on his gaudy tie. "My big chance to make good."

Carol ignored the comment. "After that I want the three of us to see Eddie Parsons. I've spoken to him, and he says he expects to be at the station until after seven tonight."

"Eddie's a key player, maybe in both cases," said Brewer. "He scared the living daylights out of Kimberley Blackland this afternoon."

Brewer had checked with Kimberley and found she would be calling into her apartment before she went back to the station after a shoot. He'd just parked when he saw Eddie Parsons coming out of the building. When Brewer went up to Kimberley's apartment he found her white and shocked. She'd finally admitted Eddie Parsons had frightened her, but she steadfastly refused to say more than that.

"By the way," Brewer said, "she *does* have a

dieffenbachia, better known as a leopard lily. Fine specimen." As Bourke pulled up at the Channel Thirteen boom gates, Brewer added, "And I've got another little nugget for you, Inspector."

Carol had promised herself not to pay attention to the way Tom Brewer always managed to give her title a sardonic fillip. She twisted around in her seat to give him an inquiring look. "About Kimberley Blackland?"

He shook his head. "Hayden Delray." He tapped his nose. "There's been a lot of talk around, and I heard a whisper about him."

Carol stopped herself from pointing out acerbically that Brewer wasn't supposed to be concerned with the Orlando case. "Delray doesn't have a record," she said evenly.

Brewer looked supremely self-satisfied. "Not as Hayden Delray, he doesn't. But try Bruce Schnell. *Then* you get a different result. I'm not surprised he changed his name."

Swinging into the visitors' car park, Bourke said over his shoulder, "I couldn't find anything under the name Bruce Schnell."

"Of course not," said Brewer complacently. "The records were sealed because he was a juvenile at the time. But one of the guys I drink with was on the case years ago. Very nasty — a pack rape of two twelve-year-old girls. Delray was there but claimed he didn't join in. He was lucky to get probation."

Carol was brutally direct. As soon as she and Brewer were seated in dark leather chairs facing

Gordon Vaughan, she said, "We have information that you and Tala Orlando had a relationship other than a business one."

His brooding, heavy-featured face remained impassive. "You should check your sources, Inspector. It isn't true."

Carol said with a note of candor, "I can see that it's understandable you wouldn't want this to become known, for business as well as personal reasons."

Vaughan leaned toward her, and she was suddenly aware of the power in his husky body. "It would be unfortunate if you were misled by someone with a hidden agenda."

"You mean Kimberley Blackland?" said Brewer. He was half-turned in his chair, one arm at ease along the back. "You sent Eddie Parsons around to scare her. Trying to shut her up?"

"What are you accusing me of — intimidation?" Vaughan glared disdain. "I guarantee that if you get Kimberley in here she'll tell you nothing of the sort ever happened."

Brewer examined his bitten fingernails. "It's not surprising that she'd deny it." He looked up. "After all, you *do* pay a fair portion of her rent on the apartment. She wouldn't want to lose that, would she?"

Carol broke in smoothly. "We have records from a local motel with charges made to Channel Thirteen."

The brown leather creaked as Vaughan sat back. "Inspector, we often provide accommodation for visiting personalities, business associates and the like. It's convenient to have them staying near the station."

Brewer's muted laugh was close to a snigger. "Got

the place, the times, the availability. Your signature every time. When we show the motel staff photos of Tala Orlando, and take you with us while we do it, what do you think they'll say?"

Vaughan bent his head for a moment, then said to Carol, "This has nothing to do with Tala's death."

Carol nodded supportively. "Nevertheless, you did mention that Tala was considering a legal separation. Was there some intention that you might eventually marry?"

"No. We were close, but marriage was never an option."

"I hope *she* knew that," said Brewer.

Vaughan flicked him a contemptuous glance. Swinging his attention back to Carol, he said, "This would only hurt Hayden and the family. Does he have to know? I'll be perfectly frank with you about Tala, but I'd appreciate discretion as far as making any of this public."

"It may be possible," she said neutrally. Carol was sure that it wasn't only possible scandal that was worrying Vaughan. At this point he hadn't signed the agreement with Orlandel for *Take the Risk,* and it would be a considerable blow to his career if the deal fell through.

"Who knew about you and Tala Orlando?"

"No one, I hope!" Vaughan showed his teeth in a rare smile.

Thinking of Nevile Carson's assertion that Vaughan had deliberately hinted at the liaison, Carol said, "You have a business arrangement with Robynne Orlando's ex-husband. Wouldn't that cause a problem with Orlandel, because of the court action?"

"Nevile Carson is developing original concepts for

us — a comedy about a psychic and a drama series about a security firm — and neither are in conflict with Orlandel's projected shows. Tala certainly wasn't thrilled to have him associated with the station, but she was always pragmatic about business matters."

Brewer broke in. "Eddie Parsons does a lot for you, doesn't he?"

Gordon Vaughan shifted in his chair. "Eddie is a valuable employee. That's basically it."

"Really?" Brewer stretched. "You sure that's all he'll tell us when we interrogate him?"

Afterwards, as they walked down the corridor, Tom Brewer said to Carol, "Good cop, bad cop. We had Vaughan on the run. We make a bloody good team, don't we?"

For once his cockiness made Carol smile. "I wouldn't go quite as far as that," she said.

Mark Bourke met them at the door to Madeline's office. "Eddie Parsons has disappeared," he said. "When I came in to interview Jim Borlie, Parsons was with him. I confirmed that we would be seeing him a bit later, and Parsons agreed to meet us at the security center on the ground floor."

"So he was called away. No big deal." Brewer yawned. "We can see him tomorrow."

"It might be a big deal," said Bourke. "Eddie's got a reputation for being reliable. He's skipped with the master keys for the entire building, plus the passwords, which change every day, for the network computer system. And his car is still in the staff parking lot."

Feeling a sudden chill of apprehension, Carol said, "Who was the last person to see him?"

"I suppose I was, together with Jim Borlie. Parsons seemed quite normal. He talked to me, then walked out the door and effectively vanished. What do you think?"

"I think we need to organize a search of the station."

It didn't take long to find him. One of the security guards searching the basement full of humming air conditioning came running back to Carol, gasping with horror.

Carol had seen death by hanging before but had never become accustomed to the nightmarish results of slow strangulation. Eddie Parsons dangled grotesquely, his toes almost touching the floor. His eyes, flecked with broken blood vessels, bulged hideously. His swollen tongue protruded from his bloated, purple-gray face.

Bourke's eyes were narrowed with revulsion. "Suicide?"

Carol didn't have to consider the question. "No," she said.

CHAPTER THIRTEEN

Eddie Parsons had lived alone in a bland suburban neighborhood ten minutes from Channel Thirteen. From the outside his house was the same as the others, neat and unremarkable. The front yard was paved, a dispirited bottle brush providing the sole vegetation.

Inside Carol found an electronic bonanza. The room in which she found Bourke resembled a command center. A console held an elaborate computer system and one wall was entirely taken up by television screens and VCRs.

"Quite a display," said Bourke. "He's got receivers tuned to police channels, he's got bugging equipment, and de-bugging equipment, directional microphones, recorders — the works."

"I want everything on his computer accessed," said Carol. "It will take a while, so put someone on it as soon as you can."

"Got it open," announced a technician crouching by a heavy metal cabinet. He tucked the slim metal picklocks into a leather case. "Wouldn't be booby-trapped, would it?"

"Hope not." Bourke pushed the handle down and swung open the door. "Bingo," he said, pointing to a squat black carrying case sitting at the bottom of the cabinet. "I believe we have a portable electric type-writer."

"I wonder why I'm not surprised," said Carol.

Bourke beckoned to a member of the team. "After it's photographed, take this straight back to the lab." He turned to Carol. "You think it's a setup, don't you?"

Carol shrugged. "Whatever we find here, I'm sure Eddie isn't Marquis."

Liz Carey, the head of the crime scene unit, poked her head around the door. "Carol, there's something that might interest you."

They followed her stocky, white-coated figure to the kitchen at the back of the house. It was immaculately clean, with all benches bare of the usual clutter of utensils. On a spotless kitchen table a row of small bottles was meticulously aligned along one edge of a cutting board. Several open gelatin capsules sat in a dish.

As a photographer took shots from different

angles, Liz grinned at Carol over the top of her wire-rimmed glasses. "We've got Valium, we've got empty capsules. What do you think of that?"

Carol bent over to scan the labels on the bottles. "This one at the end is the brand of garlic extract that Tala Orlando took every day." She straightened. "All we need is a suicide note saying, 'I killed her,' " she said sardonically, "and the case is closed in the tidiest possible way."

When she got back to her office, the preliminary post mortem report was on her desk. She took a call from Liz Carey then opened the manila folder, but before she could start reading, the phone rang again. This time it was Superintendent Edgar in an ebullient mood. "Well, Carol, looks like the Orlando case can be wrapped up. I don't want you to cut any corners, of course, but a brief statement to the media might be in order."

"I'm not convinced that Eddie Parsons murdered Tala Orlando. For one thing, he doesn't have a motive."

There was silence on the line. Carol grimaced. She didn't need this. After a moment she continued, "And if Parsons *is* the murderer, I don't believe he acted alone."

"But it is possible."

"It may be possible," Carol conceded.

Superintendent Edgar's jovial mood evaporated. "I would like a resolution in this case," he said curtly. "Keep me informed."

Carol put the receiver down hard and turned to

Eddie Parsons's post mortem. He had died from asphyxia, the noose around his neck tightened by the weight of his body. The constriction of his upper airway had led to the classic results of hanging — a grotesque bloating of the face and head because the dammed blood was unable to escape.

He had struggled. Abrasions on his finger tips showed that he had torn at the constriction around his neck, inflicting deep scratches to his skin. There were bruises on his back and abrasions under his arms. Apparently as he swung at the end of the rope his attempts to loosen the noose had bumped him against the surrounding machinery. Carol knew this did not necessarily contradict a suicide scenario — the effects of slow strangulation were so extreme that an involuntary attempt to escape was often made, however determined a person was to end his or her life.

Carol winced at the graphic photographs. If Eddie Parsons had killed himself, he'd been systematic. He had taken a length of nylon rope, fashioned a hangman's noose, gone down to the basement of Channel Thirteen and selected a heavy pipe that was strong enough to bear his weight. He'd securely attached the rope, climbed onto a metal tool box, put the noose around his neck and kicked the box away.

She read the comments on the ligature closely. The photographs clearly showed the imprinted texture of the rope in the deep groove around the circumference of his neck above the thyroid cartilage.

Eddie Parsons was strong and very fit. He wouldn't have meekly stood by while someone put a rope around his neck. He hadn't been drugged and there was no evidence of any blows to the head that would have knocked him out long enough to string him up. And his unconscious body would have been heavy and unmanageable. Bourke came in as she was visualizing scenarios that might explain these problems away.

"The typewriter matches," he said. "It was used for all the messages from Marquis. We found paper and envelopes too, but although we searched Eddie's place thoroughly, there was no note this time. Pity, it would have tied up all the loose ends."

"I don't think so, Mark."

"And Liz Carey just called. She rushed through the analysis of the stuff in the kitchen. I know the bottles you got from the Orlandel office checked out okay, but the garlic capsules here contained Valium tablets that had been ground to powder. I think there's no doubt that Tala took the diazepam believing that it was her usual morning dose of garlic extract."

Bourke leaned against a filing cabinet. "We didn't turn up any garlic extract at Tala's house. There were some vitamin tablets and a couple of herbal remedies, but no capsules."

"I'd say he took them with him. If he'd really been attending to detail, he'd have left a bottle with genuine garlic capsules."

"Nice to know he isn't perfect," Bourke said dryly. He sat down and stretched out his legs. "I've got some early info about Eddie's computer. I put the best operator we've got on it, and she says Eddie has files on a lot of people, mainly to do with the media. Most interestingly, he has information that most certainly was illegally obtained about Orlandel's future plans and strategies." Amused, he added, "And would you believe Eddie fancied himself a writer? There were notes for what looked like a screenplay or a TV script, all featuring a security guard."

"Anything else from the house? Fingerprints?"

"The typewriter had been wiped clean. No other matches from any other areas yet. Frankly, I don't expect them." He paused. "There was one other thing. Eddie had a gun cabinet. All above board — he's a licensed rifle shooter and belongs to a club. The cabinet was locked, and when we opened it we found several rifles and an empty space that may have held a shotgun. We're checking to see what's missing."

"How would you murder him, Mark, and make it look like suicide?"

Bourke gazed reflectively at his toes. "Okay, Carol, this is what I'd do. First, I'd have to get Eddie down in the basement. None of this dragging bodies around. Then I'd get behind him and half strangle him, not with wire, which would leave a distinctive mark, but with something like a stocking. If I timed it well, I'd have him groggy but not quite dead, because it would help if he could stand so that I could get my shoulder under him and lift him high enough to slip the noose over his head. With a bit of luck the rope I hanged him with would wipe out any evidence of the original strangling." He looked pleased with himself. "The perfect murder."

"It has to be a male," said Carol. "If we follow your script, even though Eddie's taken by surprise by someone he trusts, he'd violently resist being garroted. And it would take some strength to maneuver his body into position for the noose."

"Well," said Bourke cheerfully, "that removes Robynne, Kimberley and Madeline from the list."

Carol raised an eyebrow at the last name. "Madeline?"

He looked virtuous. "You've taught me never to rule anyone out."

"We *can* rule out Gordon Vaughan. He has the best of alibis. He was with me."

"Are we working on the principle that Madeline's stalker and Tala's murderer are one in the same?"

"Absolutely," said Carol decisively. "And if Eddie is an accomplice that knows too much, or tries a little blackmail, getting rid of him in a way that allows him to be blamed for everything is a sensible thing to do."

Bourke wrinkled his brow. "I don't know if I'd use *sensible* and *psychopath* in the same sentence. And Marquis is a psychopath, no doubt about it. He won't have any motive we can understand."

Carol felt the chill that emotionless cruelty always gave her. Marquis was a textbook case. She could list his qualities: a complete lack of conscience, believing that the rules never applied to him; aggressive and ruthless, concerned only with his own needs; a risk-taker with no sense of personal danger; able to mimic — but not feel — interest and consideration for others. Marquis would be unable to experience normal emotions in relationships and be totally lacking in empathy for another's suffering.

Bourke said, "I've done some checking, based on Eddie's dying between six and seven." He extended his fingers and began to tick them off. "One, Jim Borlie. After I talked to him I left to see Kimberley, so he definitely had the opportunity."

"He looks too soft — murdering Eddie is going to be hard physically."

"He might look soft. He may not be." Bourke resumed his count. "Two, Hayden Delray. He left work just before five to drive home to an empty house. There's no one to say he actually did that, or if he headed for Channel Thirteen."

"Security's been tightened at the station. That might make it difficult for him to get in undetected."

"Eddie's in charge of the security," said Bourke. "He'd know how to get someone in without any record being made." He smiled at Carol. "Now, three's my favorite. Nevile Carson. He was here at the station during the afternoon to see Vaughan. He left about four-thirty. At least, that's the time he signed out at the reception desk."

"How about Joshua Orlando?"

"Can't locate him. He's supposed to have gone up the coast surfing with a couple of friends, but no one seems to know exactly where he is."

"Find him. It's important. And get me a printout of Eddie Parsons's creative writing."

Carol stayed working in her office all day. By six o'clock she was tired and irritable. Before she left she spoke to Madeline, promising to see her the next day, called Aunt Sarah and reassured her that she was being *very* careful, and lastly had a long conversation with David, who was finding the charms of a remote sheep station somewhat limited. "Soon, darling, you can come home soon." As she put the receiver down she was comforted by the thought that her statement wasn't a soothing lie — she did believe that the end was in sight.

Bourke walked down to the car park with her. "We have an idea where Joshua Orlando may be. One of the guys he's supposed to be with called a girlfriend and said they were camping on this remote little beach on the north coast. It's four-wheel-drive territory, and I've spoken to the local cops. If he's there they'll go in and get him first thing tomorrow morning."

"Have them put him on a plane and fly him down to Sydney. I'd like you to meet the plane."

Carol drove home in a haze of fatigue. She'd slept fitfully the night before, waking at any unusual sound. She parked her car, checked everything before she opened the door, and walked rapidly down the path, her right hand in her jacket pocket cradling the weight of her gun.

Everything was normal. The light over the door banished the shadows from the front of the house, and sleepy birds muttered in the trees. Carol used the new key on the deadlock, then rapidly checked each room to make sure no windows had been forced.

She hated coming home to a house with no cats to greet her. She could imagine their unhappy indignation as they settled down for the night in alien surroundings.

She switched on the floodlight over the back deck, startling a mother possum with a baby clinging to her back. Carol put her gun carefully on the counter and grabbed a banana to give to her. She was unlocking the sliding doors to the deck when the kitchen phone rang.

She leaned over to answer it. The voice was shocking in its dear familiarity. "Carol? It's me. Sybil."

"Hi." Carol couldn't think of anything else to say.

"I'm coming back to Australia."

"Are you?"

"Is that all you're going to say?" Sybil sounded gently amused.

"I can't wait to see you," Carol said, and found that it was true.

She put down the receiver and stood staring into space.

Someone cleared his throat.

She turned around. With piercing clarity she saw the shotgun. The dull gleam of the dark metal, the rich golden brown of the wooden stock.

"You thought it was me, didn't you?"

"I thought it was you," she agreed. "If I'd spoken with Joshua Orlando, I might have known for sure."

"Yes," he said thoughtfully. "Josh is going to be a problem I'll have to do something about."

CHAPTER FOURTEEN

He moved through the sliding door and into the kitchen. He held the stock of the shotgun comfortably against his hip, the double O of the two barrels pointing unwaveringly at her face. "At this range it will blow your beautiful head off your shoulders," Nevile Carson said conversationally. He freed one hand to scoop up her gun and shove it in his jacket pocket.

His narrow face seemed so ordinary, his manner so casual. She stared at him as he let the barrels sink slowly until they pointed at her stomach. "And here it'll put a hole right through you. Disintegrate your spine and splatter your guts all over the wall behind you."

Carol remained silent. She had automatically taken a defensive stance with her left foot slightly forward, her elbows in and her hands raised to protect her body. Incredibly, although she vibrated with fear, she could recall advice from her unarmed combat training: "If you talk, do it for a specific purpose — to distract, to calm. You're not there to provide an attacker with conversation."

Carson moved the shotgun to her groin. "And here you take your pleasure. I'm sure you're very creative in love-making, but you could never imagine what this will be like. I'll ram it up you and pull both triggers." He smiled a little. "Multiple orgasm."

Carol isolated herself from the tumult of fear that shook her. *Calculate the odds.* A shotgun was a particularly devastating weapon because the concentrated blast of pellets caused catastrophic injuries at short range. Even if she could get farther away, the blast spread in a pattern that covered a wide area. And a double-barreled shotgun meant that if he missed once, he could fire again.

Nevile Carson was watching her closely. "Working out the percentages?" he asked. "Let me do it for you. I'm a hundred percent certain that you're going to die." He paused meditatively. "But will it be quick, or slow? I could put the barrels against your shoulder and blow away your arm. Then you could watch yourself bleed to death." He tilted his head to consider. "Perhaps both arms. Or, if I took great care, I believe I could blow away your bottom jaw together with half those fine white teeth."

Carol assessed the distance between them. He wasn't standing close enough for her to make any realistic attempt to disarm him. Either she could try edging closer, or she could make a run for the deck. The open glass door was so close. Wouldn't it just take an instant to be through it, across the width of the deck to vault the railing and fall into the dark bush below?

Carol kept her eyes on Carson while she visualized the deck. It was just a few strides away, but it was wide. Too wide. There was heavy wooden furniture, but she wouldn't have time to get behind it, and even if she did, he could shoot right through it, or simply walk around and fire unimpeded.

"Are you going to maintain a dignified silence, Carol?" It was the first time she had heard him say her first name, and the intimacy of his tone was somehow more shocking than the dreadful things he had been so lovingly describing to her.

Carol didn't reply. She'd decided that flight wasn't an option — he'd kill her before she made it through the door. But if she could lessen the distance between them, she had a chance, however slight.

His face darkened, the first sign of annoyance he had shown. "You've never been so quiet before when I've seen you. Always probing, asking questions. The superior Detective Inspector Carol Ashton. So cool. So good-looking." He moved the shotgun fractionally. "Just a squeeze with my finger and all that's gone, Carol. Gone forever."

"I never thought Marquis was Eddie," she said. "But then, you didn't expect me to."

"No, I didn't." Carson tilted his head interrogatively. "The typewriter and the capsules were a nice touch. I had the run of Eddie's house and I set everything up before I went to meet him at the station. I think I did an excellent job of making it look like a suicide." He smiled. "But after all, it *was* my second attempt."

"Your alibi for Tala Orlando's death fell through."

Carson raised his eyebrows in surprise. "Very good, Carol. I had Eddie lined up to fly to Perth on my ticket. No one ever checks identities on a domestic flight. But the plane was delayed, and that blew my alibi out of the water. There was no point in sending Eddie then, so after I killed Tala I went back to the airport and caught the delayed flight. I was a no-show on the second flight I'd booked under a false name — I did have genuine business appointments in Perth to cement my alibi, including a business dinner, so although Eddie was to check into my hotel under my name, I had to be there in person by early evening anyway."

Carol slid her left foot forward a little. "Did Tala know she was going to die?"

"No." His expression grew contemptuous. "For someone so good at business, Tala was such a stupid woman. She did everything I asked her to. I said I wouldn't negotiate if Hayden knew anything about it, and she agreed. I asked her to call me on my mobile once he'd left for work, and she did. When I arrived Tala had actually put a bottle of champagne in a silver bucket to celebrate." He shook his head in wonder. "She really believed that I would drop the lawsuit against Orlandel, even though we both knew she'd stolen my idea, even my title, for *Take the Risk*."

Carol eased slightly closer. "Was she easy to kill?"

"Too easy." His smile was contemptuous. "The silly bitch had obligingly taken her garlic capsules and was asleep when I rang the doorbell so I let myself in with the keys Eddie had copied for me. I woke Tala up, sweet-talked her while we drank a champagne toast to our future business relationship, and waited while the combination of Valium and alcohol worked. I half-walked half-carried her down to the garage, arranged her artistically behind the wheel, started the engine, went upstairs and washed my champagne glass, took the rest of the capsules and left."

"Eddie changed the garlic capsules for diazepam."

He nodded approval. "Eddie called in the day before with the excuse that he was there to check the new alarm system. The cleaner was getting the house ready for the dinner party, so she let him in and he switched the capsules."

How close can I get before he notices? "The cleaner was supposed to spend all morning at the house cleaning up. What would you have done if she'd been there when you arrived?"

Carson shrugged indifferently. "Changed plans. Or killed them both. I would have thought of something." He moved restlessly. "I can see what you're doing, Carol, but you can't keep me talking, much though I'm enjoying our conversation."

"It was ingenious, the way you got Eddie into the noose."

Carson laughed aloud. "Flattery, Carol? You think that will save you? Let's see how smart you are. Tell me how I did it."

"You met him in the basement with all the racket of the machinery to mask any noise you made. You got behind him and garroted him. When he was unconscious, you either used a harness, or soft rope, which you looped under his arms — it left slight abrasions. You put the other end over the pipe and hauled him upright, tying the rope to secure him in a standing position. Then you stood on something — maybe the tool box — made one great effort and heaved his head through the noose."

"I used my own tie on him — a personal gesture that he wouldn't have appreciated. Surprised him from behind and strangled him until he was half dead." He paused, then added with clinical interest, "Eddie came to, you know, just as I got the noose around his neck. He tried to get it off, but the more he struggled, the tighter it got."

Am I close enough yet? "Why did you have to kill Eddie? He'd been very useful to you."

"He was getting to be a problem, so I had to do something. And although I was paying him very well to follow orders, the cocky little bastard was starting to add little things of his own, like telling you about Borlie, instead of leaving you to find out yourself." His mouth curved in a malicious grin. "Eddie was so dumb. Can you believe he really thought I was going to use his pathetic attempts at writing in a drama series?"

"Madeline?" Carol said. She shifted her weight to her front foot.

"Tala was mainly business, though I had fun upsetting her over Robynne's supposed industrial espionage. But Madeline — she was pure fun. I can't tell you how much I enjoyed composing my letters to her, imagining her sweating and frightened." He drew himself to attention. "Now, Carol, are you going to beg for your life?"

"I don't believe I am."

His pale eyes were watching her from behind the innocuous tortoise-shell glasses. "Perhaps you won't beg for *your* life, but will you beg for David's?"

He laughed softly, gently. Carol knew he had seen the first flicker of fear on her face.

"You won't be there to save him," Carson said. "He's a beautiful boy, your only son. Plead with me, Carol. Otherwise I'll hunt him down and hurt him so much he'll ask to die. And he will . . . eventually."

It was time to give him what he wanted. "Please," Carol said. "Not David."

Delight flooded his face. "Again," he said. "Say it again."

She put her hands up to her face in a gesture of entreaty. "Please. I couldn't bear it if you hurt David. Do anything you want to me, but not him."

"This is so rewarding! I really wondered if you'd be this weak."

He was still speaking as Carol moved. She took a stride forward, her bent right arm held high. As she smacked the shotgun out of the way with her left hand, her right fist descended like a hammer to smash the bridge of his nose.

One barrel discharged with a hideous noise. Wood chips flew as the breakfast bench exploded.

Carson staggered back, still holding the shotgun, blood spurting from his shattered nose. One half his broken glasses dangled from one ear. "You bitch!"

Carol seized the end of the shotgun and forced it up to point at the ceiling. As he tried to pull it away from her, she struck him under his nose with the edge of her hand. Once. Twice. Heavy blows that snapped his head back.

He let go the stock, and she swung the shotgun around to cover him. "Just stay there. Don't move."

She was gasping, unable to catch her breath, stingingly aware that her gun was in his coat pocket, and he had forgotten it.

Nevile Carson crouched, one hand over his nose, blood pouring between his spread fingers. "I'll kill you!" he screamed.

Carol backed up. "Don't," she said. *Don't make me pull the trigger.*

With a banshee howl Nevile Carson leaped toward her. Face contorted, clawed hands extended, he was on her. "I'll tear out your throat!"

The kitchen reverberated. Blood and shreds of flesh showered the wall, the floor.

Carol stood, appalled.

CHAPTER FIFTEEN

Carol had always loved sitting in the kitchen on Saturday mornings, sipping black coffee and looking out at the eucalyptus gums where sulfur-crested cockatoos and rainbow lorikeets would cluster on hanging baskets full of Aunt Sarah's special wild bird seed formula. Now she couldn't endure being in the kitchen at all.

Professional cleaners had removed any evidence of the blood and tissue that had sprayed from Nevile Carson's body. What remained of the breakfast bar had been demolished and the lead pellets had been dug out of the wall and the holes patched. But Carol could still see his ruptured body sprawled on the floor.

"Do you mind having your coffee outside?" she said to Madeline.

Madeline put an arm around her waist. "It might be a bit cold, but I'm game."

The sunshine burnished Madeline's copper hair. Carol thought, I have to tell her about Sybil.

When they were settled in the warmest part of the deck, Madeline said, "Robynne tells me Joshua is still complaining that you dragged him back to Sydney for nothing."

"I needed him to corroborate that Nevile Carson was the source of the information that Joshua gave to Hayden. It had to come from someone who knew exactly what Orlandel was planning in the future, because it was quite accurate, which made it more convincing when Robynne was accused, even though she knew nothing about it."

Madeline tipped more sugar into her coffee. "Why didn't Josh go straight to Tala?"

"It's fairly obvious that underneath it all he was frightened of his mother. He was desperate to have his allowance restored, so he wanted the credit for telling her something important, and Nevile Carson had persuaded him that it was absolutely true that his aunt was selling information about Orlandel's projects. But he didn't want to face Tala's anger, so he told his stepfather, knowing that Hayden would immediately repeat it."

"Why keep it a secret after Tala died?" Madeline asked.

Carol gave her a wry smile. "General self-interest.

188

With the media clamoring for every little detail about the Orlando family, if this accusation got out, it would have been splashed everywhere. Hayden didn't want to alienate Robynne, who now had a third of Orlandel, so he told Joshua to keep quiet about the whole thing and he'd reinstate his allowance. For his part, Joshua didn't want to upset his aunt because he was sure he'd need her financial support in the future."

Madeline looked doubtful. "But Josh gets a third of the company, too. He's rich."

"Tala's will specified that he can't get his hands on his share until he's thirty."

"No wonder he's bitter about his stepfather's management skills." Madeline laughed. "There may not be that much of the company to inherit by the time he gets there."

Carol got up to lean against the wooden railing. The leaves of the trees drooping over the deck moved lazily, a cockatoo shrieked from a high branch. "Sybil's coming back to Australia."

Madeline looked up at her, unconcerned. "Is she? When?"

"In a few weeks." She felt obscurely irritated that Madeline was so casual about it. "That's all. I haven't discussed anything with her."

Madeline's lips curved in a smile. "I make you a promise, Carol. You'll never escape me." She laughed aloud. "You'll never *want* to escape me."

A few of the publications of
THE NAIAD PRESS, INC.
P.O. Box 10543 • Tallahassee, Florida 32302
Phone (904) 539-5965
Toll-Free Order Number: 1-800-533-1973
Mail orders welcome. Please include 15% postage.

DOUBLE BLUFF by Claire McNab. 208 pp. 7th Detective Carol Ashton Mystery.   ISBN 1-56280-096-5 $10.95

BAR GIRLS by Lauran Hoffman. 160 pp. See the movie, read the book!   ISBN 1-56280-115-5   10.95

THE FIRST TIME EVER edited by Barbara Grier & Christine Cassidy. 272 pp. Love stories by Naiad Press authors.
                                                          ISBN 1-56280-086-8   14.95

MISS PETTIBONE AND MISS McGRAW by Brenda Waters. 208 pp. A charming ghostly love story.   ISBN 1-56280-151-1   10.95

CHANGES by Jackie Calhoun. 208 pp. Involved romance and relationships.   ISBN 1-56280-083-3   10.95

FAIR PLAY by Rose Beecham. 256 pp. 3rd Amanda Valentine Mystery.   ISBN 1-56280-081-7   10.95

PAXTON COURT by Diane Salvatore. 256 pp. Erotic and wickedly funny contemporary tale about the business of learning to live together.   ISBN 1-56280-109-0   21.95

PAYBACK by Celia Cohen. 176 pp. A gripping thriller of romance, revenge and betrayal.   ISBN 1-56280-084-1   10.95

THE BEACH AFFAIR by Barbara Johnson. 224 pp. Sizzling summer romance/mystery/intrigue.   ISBN 1-56280-090-6   10.95

GETTING THERE by Robbi Sommers. 192 pp. Nobody does it like Robbi!   ISBN 1-56280-099-X   10.95

FINAL CUT by Lisa Haddock. 208 pp. 2nd Carmen Ramirez Mystery.   ISBN 1-56280-088-4   10.95

FLASHPOINT by Katherine V. Forrest. 256 pp. A Lesbian blockbuster!   ISBN 1-56280-079-5   10.95

DAUGHTERS OF A CORAL DAWN by Katherine V. Forrest. Audio Book — read by Jane Merrow.   ISBN 1-56280-110-4   16.95

CLAIRE OF THE MOON by Nicole Conn. Audio Book —Read by Marianne Hyatt.   ISBN 1-56280-113-9   16.95

FOR LOVE AND FOR LIFE: INTIMATE PORTRAITS OF
LESBIAN COUPLES by Susan Johnson. 224 pp.
ISBN 1-56280-091-4   14.95

DEVOTION by Mindy Kaplan. 192 pp. See the movie — read
the book!   ISBN 1-56280-093-0   10.95

SOMEONE TO WATCH by Jaye Maiman. 272 pp. 4th Robin
Miller Mystery.   ISBN 1-56280-095-7   10.95

GREENER THAN GRASS by Jennifer Fulton. 208 pp. A young
woman — a stranger in her bed.   ISBN 1-56280-092-2   10.95

TRAVELS WITH DIANA HUNTER by Regine Sands. Erotic
lesbian romp. Audio Book (2 cassettes)   ISBN 1-56280-107-4   16.95

CABIN FEVER by Carol Schmidt. 256 pp. Sizzling suspense
and passion.   ISBN 1-56280-089-1   10.95

THERE WILL BE NO GOODBYES by Laura DeHart Young. 192
pp. Romantic love, strength, and friendship.   ISBN 1-56280-103-1   10.95

FAULTLINE by Sheila Ortiz Taylor. 144 pp. Joyous comic
lesbian novel.   ISBN 1-56280-108-2   9.95

OPEN HOUSE by Pat Welch. 176 pp. 4th Helen Black Mystery.
ISBN 1-56280-102-3   10.95

ONCE MORE WITH FEELING by Peggy J. Herring. 240 pp.
Lighthearted, loving romantic adventure.   ISBN 1-56280-089-2   10.95

FOREVER by Evelyn Kennedy. 224 pp. Passionate romance — love
overcoming all obstacles.   ISBN 1-56280-094-9   10.95

WHISPERS by Kris Bruyer. 176 pp. Romantic ghost story
ISBN 1-56280-082-5   10.95

NIGHT SONGS by Penny Mickelbury. 224 pp. 2nd Gianna Maglione
Mystery.   ISBN 1-56280-097-3   10.95

GETTING TO THE POINT by Teresa Stores. 256 pp. Classic
southern Lesbian novel.   ISBN 1-56280-100-7   10.95

PAINTED MOON by Karin Kallmaker. 224 pp. Delicious
Kallmaker romance.   ISBN 1-56280-075-2   10.95

THE MYSTERIOUS NAIAD edited by Katherine V. Forrest &
Barbara Grier. 320 pp. Love stories by Naiad Press authors.
ISBN 1-56280-074-4   14.95

DAUGHTERS OF A CORAL DAWN by Katherine V. Forrest.
240 pp. Tenth Anniversay Edition.   ISBN 1-56280-104-X   10.95

BODY GUARD by Claire McNab. 208 pp. 6th Carol Ashton
Mystery.   ISBN 1-56280-073-6   10.95

CACTUS LOVE by Lee Lynch. 192 pp. Stories by the beloved
storyteller.   ISBN 1-56280-071-X   9.95

SECOND GUESS by Rose Beecham. 216 pp. 2nd Amanda Valentine
Mystery.   ISBN 1-56280-069-8   9.95

THE SURE THING by Melissa Hartman. 208 pp. L.A. earthquake
romance.   ISBN 1-56280-078-7   9.95

A RAGE OF MAIDENS by Lauren Wright Douglas. 240 pp. 6th Caitlin
Reece Mystery.   ISBN 1-56280-068-X   10.95

TRIPLE EXPOSURE by Jackie Calhoun. 224 pp. Romantic drama
involving many characters.   ISBN 1-56280-067-1   9.95

UP, UP AND AWAY by Catherine Ennis. 192 pp. Delightful
romance.   ISBN 1-56280-065-5   9.95

PERSONAL ADS by Robbi Sommers. 176 pp. Sizzling short
stories.   ISBN 1-56280-059-0   9.95

FLASHPOINT by Katherine V. Forrest. 256 pp. Lesbian
blockbuster!   ISBN 1-56280-043-4   22.95

CROSSWORDS by Penny Sumner. 256 pp. 2nd Victoria Cross
Mystery.   ISBN 1-56280-064-7   9.95

SWEET CHERRY WINE by Carol Schmidt. 224 pp. A novel of
suspense.   ISBN 1-56280-063-9   9.95

CERTAIN SMILES by Dorothy Tell. 160 pp. Erotic short stories.
    ISBN 1-56280-066-3   9.95

EDITED OUT by Lisa Haddock. 224 pp. 1st Carmen Ramirez
Mystery.   ISBN 1-56280-077-9   9.95

WEDNESDAY NIGHTS by Camarin Grae. 288 pp. Sexy
adventure.   ISBN 1-56280-060-4   10.95

SMOKEY O by Celia Cohen. 176 pp. Relationships on the
playing field.   ISBN 1-56280-057-4   9.95

KATHLEEN O'DONALD by Penny Hayes. 256 pp. Rose and
Kathleen find each other and employment in 1909 NYC.
    ISBN 1-56280-070-1   9.95

STAYING HOME by Elisabeth Nonas. 256 pp. Molly and Alix
want a baby . . . or do they?   ISBN 1-56280-076-0   10.95

TRUE LOVE by Jennifer Fulton. 240 pp. Six lesbians searching
for love in all the "right" places.   ISBN 1-56280-035-3   10.95

GARDENIAS WHERE THERE ARE NONE by Molleen Zanger.
176 pp. Why is Melanie inextricably drawn to the old house?
    ISBN 1-56280-056-6   9.95

KEEPING SECRETS by Penny Mickelbury. 208 pp. 1st Gianna
Maglione Mystery.   ISBN 1-56280-052-3   9.95

THE ROMANTIC NAIAD edited by Katherine V. Forrest &
Barbara Grier. 336 pp. Love stories by Naiad Press authors.
    ISBN 1-56280-054-X   14.95

UNDER MY SKIN by Jaye Maiman. 336 pp. 3rd Robin Miller
Mystery.   ISBN 1-56280-049-3.   10.95

STAY TOONED by Rhonda Dicksion. 144 pp. Cartoons — 1st
collection since *Lesbian Survival Manual*.   ISBN 1-56280-045-0   9.95

CAR POOL by Karin Kallmaker. 272pp. Lesbians on wheels
and then some!   ISBN 1-56280-048-5   10.95

NOT TELLING MOTHER: STORIES FROM A LIFE by Diane
Salvatore. 176 pp. Her 3rd novel.   ISBN 1-56280-044-2   9.95

GOBLIN MARKET by Lauren Wright Douglas. 240pp. 5th Caitlin
Reece Mystery.   ISBN 1-56280-047-7   10.95

LONG GOODBYES by Nikki Baker. 256 pp. 3rd Virginia Kelly
Mystery.   ISBN 1-56280-042-6   9.95

FRIENDS AND LOVERS by Jackie Calhoun. 224 pp. Mid-
western Lesbian lives and loves.   ISBN 1-56280-041-8   10.95

THE CAT CAME BACK by Hilary Mullins. 208 pp. Highly
praised Lesbian novel.   ISBN 1-56280-040-X   9.95

BEHIND CLOSED DOORS by Robbi Sommers. 192 pp. Hot,
erotic short stories.   ISBN 1-56280-039-6   9.95

CLAIRE OF THE MOON by Nicole Conn. 192 pp. See the
movie — read the book!   ISBN 1-56280-038-8   10.95

SILENT HEART by Claire McNab. 192 pp. Exotic Lesbian
romance.   ISBN 1-56280-036-1   10.95

HAPPY ENDINGS by Kate Brandt. 272 pp. Intimate conversations
with Lesbian authors.   ISBN 1-56280-050-7   10.95

THE SPY IN QUESTION by Amanda Kyle Williams. 256 pp.
4th Madison McGuire Mystery.   ISBN 1-56280-037-X   9.95

SAVING GRACE by Jennifer Fulton. 240 pp. Adventure and
romantic entanglement.   ISBN 1-56280-051-5   9.95

THE YEAR SEVEN by Molleen Zanger. 208 pp. Women surviving
in a new world.   ISBN 1-56280-034-5   9.95

CURIOUS WINE by Katherine V. Forrest. 176 pp. Tenth Anniver-
sary Edition. The most popular contemporary Lesbian love story.
   ISBN 1-56280-053-1   10.95
   Audio Book (2 cassettes)   ISBN 1-56280-105-8   16.95

CHAUTAUQUA by Catherine Ennis. 192 pp. Exciting, romantic
adventure.   ISBN 1-56280-032-9   9.95

A PROPER BURIAL by Pat Welch. 192 pp. 3rd Helen Black
Mystery.   ISBN 1-56280-033-7   9.95

SILVERLAKE HEAT: A Novel of Suspense by Carol Schmidt.
240 pp. Rhonda is as hot as Laney's dreams.   ISBN 1-56280-031-0   9.95

LOVE, ZENA BETH by Diane Salvatore. 224 pp. The most talked
about lesbian novel of the nineties!   ISBN 1-56280-030-2   10.95

A DOORYARD FULL OF FLOWERS by Isabel Miller. 160 pp.
Stories incl. 2 sequels to *Patience and Sarah.*   ISBN 1-56280-029-9   9.95

MURDER BY TRADITION by Katherine V. Forrest. 288 pp. 4th
Kate Delafield Mystery. ISBN 1-56280-002-7 10.95

THE EROTIC NAIAD edited by Katherine V. Forrest & Barbara
Grier. 224 pp. Love stories by Naiad Press authors.
ISBN 1-56280-026-4 13.95

DEAD CERTAIN by Claire McNab. 224 pp. 5th Carol Ashton
Mystery. ISBN 1-56280-027-2 9.95

CRAZY FOR LOVING by Jaye Maiman. 320 pp. 2nd Robin Miller
Mystery. ISBN 1-56280-025-6 9.95

STONEHURST by Barbara Johnson. 176 pp. Passionate regency
romance. ISBN 1-56280-024-8 10.95

INTRODUCING AMANDA VALENTINE by Rose Beecham.
256 pp. 1st Amanda Valentine Mystery. ISBN 1-56280-021-3 9.95

UNCERTAIN COMPANIONS by Robbi Sommers. 204 pp.
Steamy, erotic novel. ISBN 1-56280-017-5 9.95

A TIGER'S HEART by Lauren W. Douglas. 240 pp. 4th Caitlin
Reece Mystery. ISBN 1-56280-018-3 9.95

PAPERBACK ROMANCE by Karin Kallmaker. 256 pp. A
delicious romance. ISBN 1-56280-019-1 9.95

MORTON RIVER VALLEY by Lee Lynch. 304 pp. Lee Lynch
at her best! ISBN 1-56280-016-7 9.95

THE LAVENDER HOUSE MURDER by Nikki Baker. 224 pp.
2nd Virginia Kelly Mystery. ISBN 1-56280-012-4 9.95

PASSION BAY by Jennifer Fulton. 224 pp. Passionate romance,
virgin beaches, tropical skies. ISBN 1-56280-028-0 10.95

STICKS AND STONES by Jackie Calhoun. 208 pp. Contemporary
lesbian lives and loves. ISBN 1-56280-020-5 9.95
Audio Book (2 cassettes) ISBN 1-56280-106-6 16.95

DELIA IRONFOOT by Jeane Harris. 192 pp. Adventure for Delia
and Beth in the Utah mountains. ISBN 1-56280-014-0 9.95

UNDER THE SOUTHERN CROSS by Claire McNab. 192 pp.
Romantic nights Down Under. ISBN 1-56280-011-6 9.95

GRASSY FLATS by Penny Hayes. 256 pp. Lesbian romance in
the '30s. ISBN 1-56280-010-8 9.95

A SINGULAR SPY by Amanda K. Williams. 192 pp. 3rd
Madison McGuire Mystery. ISBN 1-56280-008-6 8.95

THE END OF APRIL by Penny Sumner. 240 pp. 1st Victoria
Cross Mystery. ISBN 1-56280-007-8 8.95

HOUSTON TOWN by Deborah Powell. 208 pp. A Hollis
Carpenter Mystery. ISBN 1-56280-006-X 8.95

KISS AND TELL by Robbi Sommers. 192 pp. Scorching stories
by the author of *Pleasures*. ISBN 1-56280-005-1 10.95

STILL WATERS by Pat Welch. 208 pp. 2nd Helen Black Mystery.
ISBN 0-941483-97-5 9.95

TO LOVE AGAIN by Evelyn Kennedy. 208 pp. Wildly romantic
love story.   ISBN 0-941483-85-1 9.95

IN THE GAME by Nikki Baker. 192 pp. 1st Virginia Kelly
Mystery.   ISBN 1-56280-004-3 9.95

AVALON by Mary Jane Jones. 256 pp. A Lesbian Arthurian
romance.   ISBN 0-941483-96-7 9.95

STRANDED by Camarin Grae. 320 pp. Entertaining, riveting
adventure.   ISBN 0-941483-99-1 9.95

THE DAUGHTERS OF ARTEMIS by Lauren Wright Douglas.
240 pp. 3rd Caitlin Reece Mystery.   ISBN 0-941483-95-9 9.95

CLEARWATER by Catherine Ennis. 176 pp. Romantic secrets
of a small Louisiana town.   ISBN 0-941483-65-7 8.95

THE HALLELUJAH MURDERS by Dorothy Tell. 176 pp. 2nd
Poppy Dillworth Mystery.   ISBN 0-941483-88-6 8.95

SECOND CHANCE by Jackie Calhoun. 256 pp. Contemporary
Lesbian lives and loves.   ISBN 0-941483-93-2 9.95

BENEDICTION by Diane Salvatore. 272 pp. Striking, contemporary romantic novel.   ISBN 0-941483-90-8 9.95

BLACK IRIS by Jeane Harris. 192 pp. Caroline's hidden past . . .
ISBN 0-941483-68-1 8.95

TOUCHWOOD by Karin Kallmaker. 240 pp. Loving, May/
December romance.   ISBN 0-941483-76-2 9.95

COP OUT by Claire McNab. 208 pp. 4th Carol Ashton Mystery.
ISBN 0-941483-84-3 9.95

THE BEVERLY MALIBU by Katherine V. Forrest. 288 pp. 3rd
Kate Delafield Mystery.   ISBN 0-941483-48-7 10.95

THAT OLD STUDEBAKER by Lee Lynch. 272 pp. Andy's affair
with Regina and her attachment to her beloved car.
ISBN 0-941483-82-7 9.95

PASSION'S LEGACY by Lori Paige. 224 pp. Sarah is swept into
the arms of Augusta Pym in this delightful historical romance.
ISBN 0-941483-81-9 8.95

THE PROVIDENCE FILE by Amanda Kyle Williams. 256 pp.
2nd Madison McGuire Mystery.   ISBN 0-941483-92-4 8.95

I LEFT MY HEART by Jaye Maiman. 320 pp. 1st Robin Miller
Mystery.   ISBN 0-941483-72-X 10.95

THE PRICE OF SALT by Patricia Highsmith (writing as Claire
Morgan). 288 pp. Classic lesbian novel, first issued in 1952 . . .
acknowledged by its author under her own, very famous, name.
ISBN 1-56280-003-5 9.95

SIDE BY SIDE by Isabel Miller. 256 pp. From beloved author of
Patience and Sarah.   ISBN 0-941483-77-0   9.95

STAYING POWER: LONG TERM LESBIAN COUPLES by
Susan E. Johnson. 352 pp. Joys of coupledom. ISBN 0-941-483-75-4   14.95

SLICK by Camarin Grae. 304 pp. Exotic, erotic adventure.
                                         ISBN 0-941483-74-6   9.95

NINTH LIFE by Lauren Wright Douglas. 256 pp. 2nd Caitlin
Reece Mystery.   ISBN 0-941483-50-9   8.95

PLAYERS by Robbi Sommers. 192 pp. Sizzling, erotic novel.
                                         ISBN 0-941483-73-8   9.95

MURDER AT RED ROOK RANCH by Dorothy Tell. 224 pp.
1st Poppy Dillworth Mystery.   ISBN 0-941483-80-0   8.95

LESBIAN SURVIVAL MANUAL by Rhonda Dicksion. 112 pp.
Cartoons!   ISBN 0-941483-71-1   8.95

A ROOM FULL OF WOMEN by Elisabeth Nonas. 256 pp.
Contemporary Lesbian lives.   ISBN 0-941483-69-X   9.95

THEME FOR DIVERSE INSTRUMENTS by Jane Rule. 208 pp.
Powerful romantic lesbian stories.   ISBN 0-941483-63-0   8.95

CLUB 12 by Amanda Kyle Williams. 288 pp. Espionage thriller
featuring a lesbian agent!   ISBN 0-941483-64-9   8.95

DEATH DOWN UNDER by Claire McNab. 240 pp. 3rd Carol
Ashton Mystery.   ISBN 0-941483-39-8   9.95

MONTANA FEATHERS by Penny Hayes. 256 pp. Vivian and
Elizabeth find love in frontier Montana.   ISBN 0-941483-61-4   8.95

LIFESTYLES by Jackie Calhoun. 224 pp. Contemporary Lesbian
lives and loves.   ISBN 0-941483-57-6   9.95

WILDERNESS TREK by Dorothy Tell. 192 pp. Six women on
vacation learning "new" skills.   ISBN 0-941483-60-6   8.95

MURDER BY THE BOOK by Pat Welch. 256 pp. 1st Helen
Black Mystery.   ISBN 0-941483-59-2   9.95

THERE'S SOMETHING I'VE BEEN MEANING TO TELL YOU
Ed. by Loralee MacPike. 288 pp. Gay men and lesbians coming out
to their children.   ISBN 0-941483-44-4   9.95

LIFTING BELLY by Gertrude Stein. Ed. by Rebecca Mark. 104 pp.
Erotic poetry.   ISBN 0-941483-51-7   10.95

AFTER THE FIRE by Jane Rule. 256 pp. Warm, human novel by
this incomparable author.   ISBN 0-941483-45-2   8.95

THREE WOMEN by March Hastings. 232 pp. Golden oldie. A
triangle among wealthy sophisticates.   ISBN 0-941483-43-6   8.95

PLEASURES by Robbi Sommers. 204 pp. Unprecedented
eroticism.   ISBN 0-941483-49-5   8.95

EDGEWISE by Camarin Grae. 372 pp. Spellbinding
adventure.   ISBN 0-941483-19-3   9.95

FATAL REUNION by Claire McNab. 224 pp. 2nd Carol Ashton
Mystery.   ISBN 0-941483-40-1   10.95

IN EVERY PORT by Karin Kallmaker. 228 pp. Jessica's sexy,
adventuresome travels.   ISBN 0-941483-37-7   9.95

OF LOVE AND GLORY by Evelyn Kennedy. 192 pp. Exciting
WWII romance.   ISBN 0-941483-32-0   10.95

CLICKING STONES by Nancy Tyler Glenn. 288 pp. Love
transcending time.   ISBN 0-941483-31-2   9.95

SOUTH OF THE LINE by Catherine Ennis. 216 pp. Civil War
adventure.   ISBN 0-941483-29-0   8.95

WOMAN PLUS WOMAN by Dolores Klaich. 300 pp. Supurb
Lesbian overview.   ISBN 0-941483-28-2   9.95

THE FINER GRAIN by Denise Ohio. 216 pp. Brilliant young
college lesbian novel.   ISBN 0-941483-11-8   8.95

OCTOBER OBSESSION by Meredith More. Josie's rich, secret
Lesbian life.   ISBN 0-941483-18-5   8.95

BEFORE STONEWALL: THE MAKING OF A GAY AND
LESBIAN COMMUNITY by Andrea Weiss & Greta Schiller.
96 pp., 25 illus.   ISBN 0-941483-20-7   7.95

OSTEN'S BAY by Zenobia N. Vole. 204 pp. Sizzling adventure
romance set on Bonaire.   ISBN 0-941483-15-0   8.95

LESSONS IN MURDER by Claire McNab. 216 pp. 1st Carol Ashton
Mystery.   ISBN 0-941483-14-2   9.95

YELLOWTHROAT by Penny Hayes. 240 pp. Margarita, bandit,
kidnaps Julia.   ISBN 0-941483-10-X   8.95

SAPPHISTRY: THE BOOK OF LESBIAN SEXUALITY by
Pat Califia. 3d edition, revised. 208 pp.   ISBN 0-941483-24-X   10.95

CHERISHED LOVE by Evelyn Kennedy. 192 pp. Erotic Lesbian
love story.   ISBN 0-941483-08-8   10.95

THE SECRET IN THE BIRD by Camarin Grae. 312 pp. Striking,
psychological suspense novel. ISBN 0-941483-05-3   8.95

TO THE LIGHTNING by Catherine Ennis. 208 pp. Romantic
Lesbian 'Robinson Crusoe' adventure.   ISBN 0-941483-06-1   8.95

DREAMS AND SWORDS by Katherine V. Forrest. 192 pp.
Romantic, erotic, imaginative stories.   ISBN 0-941483-03-7   8.95

MEMORY BOARD by Jane Rule. 336 pp. Memorable novel
about an aging Lesbian couple.   ISBN 0-941483-02-9   10.95

THE ALWAYS ANONYMOUS BEAST by Lauren Wright Douglas.
224 pp. 1st Caitlin Reece Mystery.
                              ISBN 0-941483-04-5   8.95

THE BLACK AND WHITE OF IT by Ann Allen Shockley.
144 pp. Short stories. ISBN 0-930044-96-7 7.95

SAY JESUS AND COME TO ME by Ann Allen Shockley. 288
pp. Contemporary romance. ISBN 0-930044-98-3 8.95

MURDER AT THE NIGHTWOOD BAR by Katherine V. Forrest.
240 pp. 2nd Kate Delafield Mystery. ISBN 0-930044-92-4 10.95

WINGED DANCER by Camarin Grae. 228 pp. Erotic Lesbian
adventure story. ISBN 0-930044-88-6 8.95

PAZ by Camarin Grae. 336 pp. Romantic Lesbian adventurer
with the power to change the world. ISBN 0-930044-89-4 8.95

SOUL SNATCHER by Camarin Grae. 224 pp. A puzzle, an
adventure, a mystery — Lesbian romance. ISBN 0-930044-90-8 8.95

THE LOVE OF GOOD WOMEN by Isabel Miller. 224 pp.
Long-awaited new novel by the author of the beloved *Patience
and Sarah*. ISBN 0-930044-81-9 8.95

THE HOUSE AT PELHAM FALLS by Brenda Weathers. 240
pp. Suspenseful Lesbian ghost story. ISBN 0-930044-79-7 7.95

HOME IN YOUR HANDS by Lee Lynch. 240 pp. More stories
from the author of *Old Dyke Tales*. ISBN 0-930044-80-0 7.95

PEMBROKE PARK by Michelle Martin. 256 pp. Derring-do
and daring romance in Regency England. ISBN 0-930044-77-0 7.95

THE LONG TRAIL by Penny Hayes. 248 pp. Vivid adventures
of two women in love in the old west. ISBN 0-930044-76-2 8.95

AN EMERGENCE OF GREEN by Katherine V. Forrest. 288
pp. Powerful novel of sexual discovery. ISBN 0-930044-69-X 10.95

THE LESBIAN PERIODICALS INDEX edited by Claire Potter.
432 pp. Author & subject index. ISBN 0-930044-74-6 12.95

DESERT OF THE HEART by Jane Rule. 224 pp. A classic;
basis for the movie *Desert Hearts*. ISBN 0-930044-73-8 10.95

TORCHLIGHT TO VALHALLA by Gale Wilhelm. 128 pp.
Classic novel by a great Lesbian writer. ISBN 0-930044-68-1 7.95

LESBIAN NUNS: BREAKING SILENCE edited by Rosemary
Curb and Nancy Manahan. 432 pp. Unprecedented autobiographies
of religious life. ISBN 0-930044-62-2 9.95

THE SWASHBUCKLER by Lee Lynch. 288 pp. Colorful novel
set in Greenwich Village in the sixties. ISBN 0-930044-66-5 8.95

These are just a few of the many Naiad Press titles — we are the oldest and largest lesbian/feminist publishing company in the world. Please request a complete catalog. We offer personal service; we encourage and welcome direct mail orders from individuals who have limited access to bookstores carrying our publications.